MW00943853

CAUGHT DEAD HANDED

LYNDSEY COLE

CAUGHT DEAD HANDED

A Hooked & Cooked Cozy Mystery

by Lyndsey Cole

CONNECT WITH ME:

LYNDSEY@LYNDSEYCOLEBOOKS.COM

www.facebook.com/LyndseyColeAuthor

BOOK DESCRIPTION

When Hannah Holiday gets kissed by the sweetest Moodle she's ever seen, she finds herself exactly where she does not want to be...in the middle of a messy custody battle for the Maltese-Poodle mix. Hannah is pulled right into the thick of helping her sister's friend as the custody conflict boils over into a deadly disaster.

While Hannah's cook, Meg, goes on a baking spree mixing up one new tasty treat after another at The Fishy Dish, a photoshoot with swimsuit models stirs the quiet town of Hooks Harbor. The suspects are able to drown their troubles with coffee, strawberry tarts, and lemon squares at the snack bar, bringing them right into Hannah's business and life.

With each suspect pointing a finger at another, Hannah needs answers, especially after one suspect's alibi sticks like caramel. The heat gets turned to high when her sister's friend looks like the guilty suspect and her life is put on the line. Along with Hannah's.

It will take more than the adorable Moodle and Petunia, the potbelly pig, to save Hannah from becoming fish bait.

CHAPTER 1

"This is exactly what we all need on a warm summer night." Hannah handed a frozen strawberry daiquiri to her sister, Ruby, and Ruby's friend, Juliette.

Juliette accepted the frozen drink with her free hand while her ten-pound Moodle, Maisy, lay in the crux of her other arm. "This will taste delish after losing those one hundred and sixty-five pounds."

Hannah lowered her head and peered at Juliette. Her eyes traveled up and down Juliette's sleek body before she remembered to shut her mouth that had opened at the thought of anyone losing that much weight. She remained frozen to the spot in front of Juliette. Staring.

"Oh, Jules," Ruby said, "Hannah didn't know you when you had all that extra weight."

Hannah continued to stare at Juliette. With her slim, athletic body, without a trace of any unwanted pounds, it was impossible for Hannah to imagine Juliette having an additional one hundred plus pounds on her body.

Ruby burst out laughing, almost spilling the frozen drink on Hannah's white porch floor. "I can't keep a straight face when

Hannah looks like you just announced something more shocking than saying an alligator was climbing up those porch steps."

Juliette sipped her drink. "Sorry, Hannah. I can't resist that line with new people."

"What are you two talking about? Losing that much weight is admirable. It's just, well, I can't imagine you without your drop-dead gorgeous model looks."

"Oh, these looks never changed." Juliette fluffed her long brown hair. "That weight? When I kicked out my no good, cheating, nearly ex-husband, Harold Chandler the la-di-da Third, *he* got to keep his one hundred and sixty-five pounds for himself and his new sweetheart."

Hannah didn't miss the disgust lacing Juliette's words. "Oh." She chuckled as she sank onto the chair between Ruby and Juliette. "Your husband weighs a hundred and sixty-five pounds. I get it now."

"So," Ruby began but had to stop to get her laughing under control. "Now that you're up to speed, Hannah, Juliette's soon-to-be ex is in town for a swimsuit photoshoot this weekend." She wiped the laughter tears from her eyes.

"I can't believe I made all the arrangements six months ago, then, *boom*, he left me for his new and improved twenty-something model." Juliette had already slugged down three quarters of her drink. "And it's in our agreement that Maisy will be part of the shoot so I have to stick around to chaperone." She drained her glass and held it toward Hannah. "Any more of these?"

Hannah filled Juliette's glass from the pitcher sitting on the small porch table.

Juliette stroked Maisy. "We're in a custody battle over her and I don't dare let her out of my sight for one second or that no-good schemer will figure out a way to convince the judge that I'm unstable or something."

Hannah had a sinking feeling that Ruby's suggestion for a girl's night together was turning into some kind of favor request. She knew how her sister liked to sneak up with a request instead of just being upfront about it.

"So, Hannah, what are your plans this weekend?" Ruby asked.

"I...uh..." She wracked her brain and came up with nothing. And she couldn't use the excuse of hanging out with her boyfriend, Cal, since he was gone fishing for the weekend. "I," she began again, "guess I don't have anything planned."

"Good. It's settled, then. As the event coordinator at the Paradise Inn, I'm in charge of the photo event and I won't be able to keep Juliette company constantly." Ruby swiveled to face Hannah directly. "She really needs another pair of eyes on Maisy so Harold can't do anything sleazy."

Hannah looked at Maisy curled up in Juliette's lap, and the little Moodle—a Maltese-Poodle cross—met Hannah's eyes with a big soulful gaze. Hannah could never resist a dog in need but she wasn't sure she wanted to be in the middle of an ugly custody battle. Over a dog. "Tell me about Maisy."

At the sound of her name, Maisy raised her head and pulled the edges of her lips back into a funny doggy smile. Hannah's heart melted. Juliette lifted Maisy up so she was face to face with her dog. "My wittle Maisy? Such a good wittle girl, aren't you?"

Great. Baby talk was not part of Hannah's vocabulary when it came to the dog world. She had no trouble talking to her dogs, Nellie and Patches, who were sprawled on the porch oblivious to the conversation, but she used her normal voice.

"Here, Hannah." Juliette plopped Maisy on Hannah's lap. "I adopted Maisy about a year ago from a rescue shelter and she bonded to me immediately. I used to go to some of Harold's photoshoots and his models usually fell in love with her so she ended up as a regular in his commercial photos. I don't think he really cares about her except for how she helps him sell his work. That's why we're in this battle."

Maisy licked Hannah's cheek.

Juliette laughed. "She likes you, Hannah. Maisy is very particular and she doesn't kiss just anyone."

Hannah smiled as Maisy made herself comfy on her lap. She knew she'd been tricked into helping this adorable dog. "Okay. I'll help."

Ruby and Juliette exchanged a look which Hannah didn't miss. "I know how you operate, Ruby, you two had this whole thing planned. Suggest a relaxing setting, add in a delicious alcoholic drink, and to top it all off, you bring an adorable dog." Hannah shook her head. "You must be feeling proud of yourself for pulling this off so smoothly."

Ruby drained the last bit of her strawberry daiquiri. "Yup, especially when you invited us here to your incredible new cottage overlooking the ocean and made the drinks, too! All we had to do was show up with an irresistible Maisy."

Hannah knew when she'd been beaten, but watching Maisy while the dog worked might prove to be an interesting experience.

"There is one more thing," Juliette said.

Hannah rolled her eyes. "Don't push your luck."

"There's been a last-minute request for a pig for this photoshoot." Juliette held up her hands. "Don't ask me why, but it could fit in perfectly. Before you say anything, here's what I'm thinking. If you hire out Petunia, that's her name, right?"

Hannah nodded. Petunia, the potbelly pig that she inherited from a previous guest, now lived happily in a pen behind Ruby's house.

"If you hire her out, it will make more sense for you to be at the photoshoot with me. Otherwise, Harold might say you can't hang around."

"What will she have to do? She's not exactly well-trained. Petunia's cute and likes to walk on a leash but she doesn't know any tricks, and if she gets a bit of freedom, she could cause some problems."

"That sounds perfect. She'll be in the background. Ruby said she doesn't mind wearing sunglasses and a hat?"

"That's true, and she does love to be the center of attention." Juliette held up her glass. "Cheers to a plan coming together! I feel better about this weekend already."

Hannah and Ruby clinked their glasses against Juliette's.

"Who else will be at the shoot?" Hannah asked. She leaned back and stretched out her legs. The drink was finally kicking in and she felt herself relax.

"That's the part I've been dreading." Juliette scowled. "Besides having to see Harold, he has a new little blonde bombshell named Monique as his model du jour, and the last thing I want is to have to interact with *her*. She probably can't even string a coherent sentence together." Juliette crossed her right leg over her left knee and bounced her foot. "Just thinking about them makes my blood boil."

Nellie, Hannah's golden retriever mix, put her head on Juliette's lap. She had a special sense for knowing when someone needed some doggy loving. "Aren't you just the sweetest girl?" Juliette stroked Nellie's soft fur. Maisy raised her head and watched.

"Uh-oh, someone's getting jealous," Hannah observed. Maisy put her front feet on the arm of Hannah's chair and vigorously wagged her tail. She stretched one paw to tap Nellie's nose.

"I don't think she's jealous," Juliette said. "She found a new friend."

Of course, Patches, Hanna's beagle, not wanting to be left out, sat and looked at Maisy with his sad brown eyes.

"How about a walk to the beach so these dogs can get to know each other a little better," Hannah suggested. She also thought it might be a good chance to move them toward their cars so she could get back to her cottage for some peace and quiet before she went to bed. All of a sudden, she didn't have the whole weekend to herself like she had planned.

They walked down the path past Hannah's guest cottages and snack bar. The tide was out but it still had a restful rhythm that always soothed Hannah. A few early stars sprinkled light across the sky and reflected on the ocean.

"This is gorgeous." With her eyes closed, Juliette spread her arms wide, inhaling deeply. "I could settle down in a place like this to put my life back together once I'm completely done with Harold. I hate how he keeps popping back into my life like a bad nightmare. I wish he'd disappear once and for all."

"Be careful what you wish for, Juliette," Ruby said. "Your nice monthly income would disappear, too. At least Harold is good for that."

Both Juliette and Ruby laughed.

Hannah felt a knot in her stomach as she worried about what she'd agreed to get involved in for her weekend.

CHAPTER 2

Saturday blew in with a dense fog that promised to burn off by mid-morning. At least that was what the weather forecast predicted.

Hannah headed to the beach for her early morning walk with Nellie and Patches. It was usually her favorite time of day since the beach was deserted and peaceful. But with her conversation from the night before swirling through her brain, she decided to head to Jack's house instead.

He was the first person she met when she inherited her Great Aunt Caroline's cottages and snack bar, and even though fifty or so years separated them, she knew she could count on him for advice. As long as she looked beyond his crotchety style.

The dogs knew the path from the beach through the rocks and darted ahead of Hannah, straight to Jack's door. Hannah opened the door and the two dogs made a beeline to the kitchen.

"Don't you believe in knocking?" Jack's gruff voice asked.

"If you're talking to Nellie and Patches, the answer is, 'no', they don't knock. If you're talking to me, the answer is also 'no' since I'm being neighborly and checking in on you this morning. Is coffee ready?"

Jack puttered around his kitchen, muttering under his breath about boundaries and the unmannered younger generation. He set a second mug in front of Hannah, filled it with his steaming strong coffee, and sat across from her. "You have that look of yours that something is on your mind." He pushed a plate of raspberry coffee cake slices closer to Hannah. "Help yourself."

Hannah sighed. "I'm not sure what's going on."

"But?" Jack bit into a slice of coffee cake. "Meg made this. It's a new recipe she's tinkering with. I think she wants to surprise you when she makes it for The Fishy Dish, so don't tell her I gave you a sample."

Eating delayed talking so Hannah helped herself. They ate in a comfortable silence.

"Okay, what's on your mind, Hannah?"

"Ruby brought a friend over last night—Juliette. She's in the middle of a custody battle. Over a dog."

Jack's thick white brows shot up. "That's a thing? Fighting over a dog? There are plenty of dogs that need homes. One of them keeps the dog and the other one adopts another one. Problem solved." Jack wiped his hands together for emphasis.

"Apparently, Juliette's soon-to-be-ex uses this dog in his photoshoots but the dog is bonded to Juliette. He wants the dog to help him sell his work but she loves the dog. I know, it's crazy but here's the problem. Juliette is chaperoning Maisy this weekend while her almost-ex is doing a swimsuit commercial shoot. She wants me to help her and they also want to use Petunia in the photos."

"Huh. Beautiful girls in bikinis? I wouldn't mind helping." Jack's eye twinkled with delight.

"Oh, please, Jack. That's just a little creepy."

"What? I have a very artistic mind. I can appreciate beauty."

She ignored his comments. "The problem is that I don't want to be in the middle of two people having a fight but I met Maisy and she's adorable. I'd hate for anything to happen to her."

"You and your soft spot for anything with four legs. So, you can't say no."

"Right. I can't say no, but the whole thing gives me a bad feeling." Hannah finished her coffee. "No omelet this morning? I expected to hear the smoke alarm when I walked in," she teased.

"I'm out of eggs. My girls are on strike and haven't been laying."

"Your *girls?* I like that, Jack. You and your Rhode Island Reds make a sweet little family. Maybe Harold will want a few chickens in one of his photoshoots. Do you think they would tolerate sunglasses and a visor?"

"Hey. That's a great idea. Can you put a word in for me?"

Hannah stood. "Sure, but I'm not sure I'll have any influence."

Nellie and Patches got the message that it was time to go and they waited at the door for Hannah to catch up.

With her hand on the doorknob, Jack gave Hannah a last piece of advice. "Don't forget to be surprised when Meg lets you try her new recipe. If she finds out I gave you a sample, she won't let me be her tester anymore."

Hannah pulled the door just as Jack's daughter, Deputy Pam Larsen, pushed on it, almost causing Hannah to tumble backwards. Nellie and Patches wagged happily at another person to offer ear rubs.

"Hannah." Pam nodded her greeting as she lavished attention on the two dogs.

"Pam." The exchange between the two women was short but courteous. Hannah knew she was not on Pam's favorite person list, not that many people were.

"The coffee's still hot, Pam," Jack called from the kitchen.

"I was hoping you'd have some but I can't stay for long." She held up her travel mug. "I'm on my way to the Paradise Inn. One of the entitled guests claims that there was an attempt to kidnap her dog." Pam rolled her eyes.

Hannah couldn't believe her ears. "When did this happen?"

Pam flicked her wrist. "Oh, a half hour ago."

Jack carried his coffee pot out and filled Pam's mug. "Hannah met someone staying there with a dog in the middle of a custody battle. Maybe that's the one."

Pam's eyes narrowed. "You know something about this?"

"Not a kidnapping attempt, but Ruby's friend is going through a messy divorce and the dog seems to be in the middle."

"Figures. These rich folks…"

Pam didn't finish her thought but Hannah suspected she wasn't impressed with the behavior of some of the tourists that spent time in Hooks Harbor. She probably had good reason, but still, without the tourists, Hooks Harbor wouldn't be a thriving coastal Maine town.

Hannah scooched herself around Pam in an effort to extricate herself from the situation, only to see Ruby rushing toward Jack's house with her daughter, Olivia, who clung onto her teddy bear, Theodore, with an iron grip. "Hannah, I've just gotten terrible news," she huffed as soon as she was close enough. "I have to go to the Inn. Juliette's a complete mess. Can you keep an eye on Olivia?"

Olivia already had herself squished between the two dogs, whispering a six-year-old's secret in Nellie's ear. Hannah loved her niece but it was almost impossible to get any work done while keeping an eye on her. She tilted her head and looked at Jack with what she hoped was her best, can-you-please-please-please-help-me-out, look.

"Juliette?" Pam asked, her eyes narrowed into a glare. "How do you know her?"

Ruby ran her fingers through her short hair. "She's just a friend."

"Staying at the Paradise Inn. Where you work." Pam waited with one hand on her hip. "Are you sure you don't have anything else to tell me about her?"

"She called me in tears about a half hour ago. I don't know

what happened." Ruby's gaze traveled from Pam to Hannah to Jack. "Did something happen to Juliette?"

"Someone tried to kidnap Maisy," Hannah blurted out before Pam could silence her.

"This is getting more and more interesting. You both seem to know this hysterical woman *and* the dog," Pam said. "Fill me in." She sipped her travel mug.

Ruby shifted from one foot to the other. "I need to get to work. Hannah, can you tell Officer Larson about Juliette and Maisy?"

"Sure. And don't worry about Olivia. Between me, Jack, and Samantha, we'll have her covered."

"Thank you." Ruby turned toward her house. "Will you still be able to come to the Inn later with Petunia?"

"I'll be there." Hannah shooed Ruby on her way with a wave of her hand.

"I can't wait to hear all the details. How about we sit down while I drink my coffee?" Pam walked into Jack's kitchen without waiting for a response.

Hannah rolled her eyes at Jack.

Jack stayed outside with Olivia and the dogs.

Hannah sat in the same seat she had been in earlier. Her fingernails tapped a staccato rhythm on Jack's well-worn pine kitchen table. Her day had barely begun but she already felt overwhelmed with having Olivia for the day, jumping into a dog custody situation that looked to be escalating from a mess to a disaster, and finding time for her normal responsibilities at The Fishy Dish and her rental cottages. She shook her head.

Pam licked raspberry off her finger as if *she* didn't have a care in the world. "That was delicious. Where did my dad get this coffee cake?"

"Um, Meg's new recipe. But you didn't hear it from me." Hannah shifted in her chair. "Listen, Pam, all I know about the dog situation is that Juliette and her soon-to-be-ex-husband, Harold, are fighting over custody of Maisy. The dog. Maisy's a sweet little Moodle stuck in the middle of a photographer that only wants her to use in his photoshoots and Juliette, who wants the best for the dog she rescued from a shelter."

Pam put her hand up. "You lost me at 'A Moodle'?"

"Apparently, that's what you call a Maltese crossed with a Poodle. Anyway, Juliette did express concern that Harold might try to undermine her in order to get custody. Maybe that's what this attempted kidnapping is all about."

"And, just for fun, what's Petunia got to do with all this?"

"They want a pig in the background of some of the photos." Hannah shrugged. "That's really all I know."

"But, you'll be at the Paradise Inn later with Petunia?"

"I did agree to bring Petunia and help Juliette keep an eye on Maisy."

"Good." Pam stood. "I'll be on my way."

Good? Hannah wondered what *that* was supposed to mean. Pam usually wanted Hannah as far away as possible from any crime, dog related or otherwise.

Hannah waited several minutes, just to be on the safe side that Pam was gone, before she ventured outside.

"...and Nellie loves me best, then Theodore, then Patches," Olivia's small voice explained to Jack.

"Where do *I* fit in?" he asked.

Olivia put her finger over her lips and scrunched her eyes. "I'll ask Nellie." She lifted the dog's ear and whispered, then looked back up at Jack. "Well, Nellie loves Hannah and then you. But she loves me best," Olivia emphasized again.

Hannah smiled, happy that Olivia had Nellie to watch over her, too. They were inseparable whenever Olivia visited. Hannah didn't doubt that Nellie would risk her own life to protect the little girl if necessary.

CHAPTER 3

M eg, Hannah's cook at The Fishy Dish and right-hand helper for miscellaneous jobs, shot her a killer glare when Hannah finally arrived in the kitchen of the snack bar. "Did Jack let you try my new raspberry coffee cake? I know you always stop at his house in the morning for coffee." She pointed her wooden spoon at Hannah like it was a weapon.

Hannah paused just inside the door. Was this a trick question? "Oh, that was *your* baking?" Hannah looked away from Meg and brushed an imaginary crumb off the counter, hoping her evasive reply wasn't too obvious.

Meg, with one hand on her hip and the wooden spoon now waving in front of her, forced Hannah to look at her. "Yes, that was my new secret raspberry coffee cake recipe. And if he gave you a piece, I can bet today's profits that he told you where it came from. Jack can keep secrets but not from you."

"All right, he told me but he made me swear not to let you know. What's the big deal? It was absolutely delicious."

Meg let the edges of her lips curl up slightly. The praise was working.

"And, Pam had a piece, too. She practically swooned on Jack's floor," Hannah added as she pretended to buckle at her knees.

Meg chuckled. "Yeah, right. Pam and swooning will never go together in the same sentence, but nice try. *You're* off the hook, but Jack's going to hear about this." She returned her attention back to stirring her clam chowder. "Are you looking forward to a nice quiet weekend?"

"I was until last night." Hannah got cabbage, carrots, onions, and mayo out for a big batch of coleslaw. The food processor made quick work of the vegetables and the noise made it impossible for Meg to pry.

A finger attached to Meg's arm reached over and hit the *off* button. "I think your cabbage is well shredded. What happened last night?"

Hannah explained about the situation with Juliette, her soon-to-be-ex-husband, Harold, and the ten-pound Moodle named Maisy; plus the photoshoot and the dog-napping attempt.

"That sounds awful for Ruby's friend, but why does that affect *your* weekend?"

"Maisy has the most adorable brown eyes, waggy tail, and," Hannah held out both hands palm-up in front of her, "she gave me a kiss."

Meg rolled her own eyes. "Don't you have enough dogs with Nellie and now with Patches becoming a permanent resident here?"

"I'm not adopting Maisy. It's nothing like that." Hannah dumped the cabbage and carrots into a big bowl, added a generous scoop of mayo, and started to stir the coleslaw. "Juliette wants another pair of eyes on Maisy while she's with Harold for the photoshoot. And, in light of this dog-napping attempt, I can see why."

"Won't that look a bit weird to her almost-ex? Having a random person show up? I wouldn't want any strangers hanging around if I was one of the models prancing around in a tiny bit of fabric."

"I'm bringing Petunia as a background prop so that will be my cover."

Meg laughed. "You'll have to give her a bath first. I saw that area you made for her behind Ruby's house and she loves to enjoy a good roll in the muddy corner."

"Good point. I never even thought of that. I also need to find her sunglasses and sunhat. Once she's all dressed up, I suspect she'll steal the show and be the star of the photoshoot." Hannah slid the bowl of coleslaw into the refrigerator just as Samantha Featherstone pranced into the kitchen.

"Am I late? What did I miss? My super sleuthing senses have picked up a vibe of something out of the ordinary happening today." Samantha, all five feet two inches of her petite eightyish year old body stood at attention eyeing Meg and Hannah with ice blue twinkling eyes that perfectly matched her rayon blouse.

"Just so long as nothing goes wrong, I guess it could be interesting." Meg ignored Samantha's enthusiasm and turned the burner under the chowder to low. She began the big daily task of hand cutting both white and sweet potatoes for fries.

Samantha's nose was in the air. "I knew something was up the minute I smelled the clam chowder. What's going to go wrong?"

Meg frowned at her. "That doesn't even make any sense. You took a wild guess but I'll let Hannah explain the latest drama that dropped in her lap."

Samantha clapped her hands. "Terrific. I'm ready for some good old fashioned drama around here. We haven't had anything fun happen for weeks. Does it have anything to do with the swimsuit shoot?"

Hannah stared at Samantha. "How do you know about that?"

"Well, I saw a flyer last week that put out a call for models." Her eyes moved from Hannah to Meg. "I'm going to the walk-in audition later." She fluffed up her short silver curls and twisted her shoulders back and forth in an attempt to look like she could walk a runway with grace.

Meg covered her mouth when a fit of laughter threatened to send her from the kitchen.

Hannah forced her own mouth to behave.

"What?" Samantha's eyebrows rose. "You two don't think I've still got it?"

"You and Petunia might be the hit of the day," Meg managed to spurt out between her laughing.

"Petunia? What a great idea. How about I help you give her a makeover and I'll arrive with that adorable potbelly pig. It will be sure to get me noticed." Samantha helped herself to the coffee that Meg always made first thing when she arrived, which had to be lukewarm, at best, by now.

Hannah washed and dried her hands and wondered if it was the right kind of attention that Samantha would get. "I like your idea. Once we get through the lunch rush, we'll get Petunia all cleaned up and I'll tell you about the rest of the drama at the swimsuit event. But now, I hear some customers out front so I'll see to that."

Hannah walked to the front of The Fishy Dish where a man and a young blonde woman were looking over the menu on the blackboard over the counter.

"Oh, Harold." The young woman swatted his hand. "Don't let anyone catch you doing that when we're doing the photoshoot. I don't want people to think I'm sleeping with you just to get this modeling job." She giggled and leaned against the man.

Well, this morning was only getting more and more interesting, Hannah told herself. She had a strong suspicion that this mustached Harold must be Juliette's almost-ex-husband—Harold Chandler III—and the blonde had to be Monique.

"Can I help you?" Hannah asked in her friendliest voice.

"This is just the cutest little snack bar I've ever seen," gushed the blonde. "I'll have, ah, let me think." She studied the menu for a bit longer as she chewed on her fingernail. "A haddock sandwich, baked, no mayo, and no bread." She giggled again. "I guess that's not a sandwich is it, Harold?"

"No, Monique. I think you just ordered plain baked haddock. I'll have the fried fish platter." He studied Hannah's face, making her a bit uneasy from the extreme attention. "We'll be sitting outside over there." He pointed to one of the picnic tables under a red umbrella. A big camera and a bag covered half the table, which helped to confirm Hannah's suspicion about his identity.

"I'll bring it out when it's ready. There are drinks in the cooler." Hannah pointed to the side of the snack bar where a cooler held a large assortment of cold drinks.

Monique strutted to the cooler. She talked to herself debating the choices but finally grabbed a water. "What do you want, Harold?"

"Anything cold." He was already half way to the table outside. He picked up his camera and moved closer to the beach and the ocean. "Come over here, Monique. I'll get a few shots before we eat."

After Hannah gave Meg the order, she busied herself outside so she could keep an eye on the couple. Monique threw her flimsy sundress on the table. She paused, facing the ocean, before she ran across the sand in her red bikini with her blonde hair sailing behind her tan shoulders. She kept a safe distance from the waves rushing in and out. Harold moved around, adjusting his camera and even kneeling in the sand for a different angle.

Hannah was intrigued. Showing up later at the Inn with Samantha and Petunia to watch Harold in action might turn out to be interesting after all. As long as any drama between Harold and Juliette was left outside, she reminded herself.

"Ouch!" Monique yelled when Harold took her hand in his to pull her back to the table.

He turned her hand over and examined it. "What happened?"

A big white bandage covered the tender area between Monique's thumb and forefinger.

She pulled her hand away. "Oh, nothing. I cut myself."

Hannah hated to drag herself away from this interaction, but she had to get their food. As soon as she entered the kitchen, both Meg and Samantha practically pounced on her.

Meg pulled Hannah away from the kitchen door. "What's going on outside?"

"Who are those people?" Samantha asked as she peeked through the door. Her eyes were round saucers when she turned back toward Hannah. "She looks like a model. Is that the swimsuit photographer?"

"That's my guess." Hannah picked up the two plates, balanced them expertly, and used her hip to push her way through the door.

Harold and Monique were settling themselves across from each other at the table when Hannah approached.

"Ugh. What's this on the seat?" Monique asked Harold.

As if on cue, a seagull landed near the table.

"Probably seagull poop. Sit on a towel." At least Harold had some common sense.

Hannah set the two trays in front of them. "Here you go. One award-winning fried fish platter which is our best seller, and one haddock sandwich, baked, no mayo, and no bread." Hannah smiled at Monique. "I wish I had your will power."

Monique flicked her wrist. "It's not so hard." Monique stared at Harold's fried fish platter overflowing with crispy haddock, coleslaw, and a mountain of French fries. "You're gonna eat all that?" She helped herself to one of the fries.

Harold used the opportunity to grab Monique's hand and pull the bandage off, revealing an ugly red wound. "This doesn't look like you cut yourself." He tossed her hand aside.

Hannah moved back a few steps to clear off a different table.

She remained within hearing distance behind Harold but facing Monique.

Deep red colored Monique's cheeks. She lowered her eyes away from Harold.

"It looked like a puncture wound, like you were bitten."

"That stupid dog you use in the photoshoots bit me." Monique taped the bandage over the wound and looked down at her baked fish.

"Well, there is a solution to that problem, dear." Harold's voice held an angry jeer.

"I was hoping you'd get rid of her." Monique, obviously, did not pick up on Harold's tone. She nibbled a small bit of fish off her fork.

Harold leaned his head across the table, closer to Monique. "That was *not* what I was suggesting. Maisy is the most important part of my work as far as my customers are concerned. And I intend to keep my customers happy." He returned to his original position and stabbed a piece of fried haddock. "Models are as plentiful as the sand on this beach."

Monique's mouth dropped open. "Is that why you brought Gwen along, too?"

Hannah couldn't see Harold's face but she didn't miss how he draped one ankle over the other and calmly began eating. She suspected Monique's position as one of Harold's models and as his new girlfriend might not be as strong as she hoped it was.

But the bigger question was: Why did Maisy bite Monique? Was she the attempted dog-napper? Juliette was bound to insist that Monique be removed from Maisy's life if that was the case.

19

CHAPTER 4

By the time the lunch rush was over at The Fishy Dish, Hannah and Samantha headed to Ruby's house to give Petunia her makeover.

Samantha beamed from ear to ear with the excitement of the project.

Hannah forced herself to make the most of what she considered to be, at best, an unpleasant task.

Petunia grunted and squealed when they came into her view. Her ears twitched forward and she stomped her feet, ready for any adventure.

"I'll get some treats to keep Petunia busy if you drag the hose into her pen," Hannah told Samantha.

It was slim pickings in Ruby's kitchen but Hannah found some leftover plain popcorn which was Petunia's favorite treat. That, along with apple peels, were sure to please the potbelly pig. She threw the treats and a few homemade dog bones in a basket to bring into the pen along with Petunia's sunhat and sunglasses.

Samantha had the hose ready to go. While she waited for Hannah to bring the treats, she crooned and scratched behind Petunia's ears. "That's the spot, isn't it, pretty girl?"

Petunia's sensitive nose tested the air, found the scent hidden in the basket, and charged at Hannah, nosed the basket, and began devouring the spilled contents.

"This is as good a spot as any." Samantha turned on the hose to a gentle spray and began cleaning the mud off Petunia's skin with an old brush.

While Samantha scrubbed and scratched and Petunia grunted, groaned, and gobbled down the treats, Hannah got the halter ready. "Once she's clean, I'll get this on so she doesn't head back into her muddy corner for a nice roll."

With the mud washed away, Petunia stepped right into the halter with barely a push on her hind end. Hannah clipped on the leash. Petunia looked from Hannah to Samantha as if to say, *okay, what's next for fun?*

"I think all of Petunia's mud splattered on me," Samantha said. "I need to do my own makeover. Want me to come back and pick you up in an hour?"

"Sure. I'll get Olivia and she can help me walk Petunia and the dogs. Jack can probably use a break from babysitting."

The walk to Jack's house wasn't far and Petunia strutted proudly next to Hannah. Maybe being in front of a camera was exactly what would bring out her dynamic personality.

Hannah took a deep breath to relax the unsettled feeling about this whole photography thing. She had to be supportive for Ruby's sake since the success, or failure, of this event would reflect directly on her sister.

A happy shriek pierced the air when Olivia spotted Hannah. She jumped with excitement at the opportunity to walk on the beach leading her potbelly pig while Nellie and Patches chased seagulls. The warm sand buried Hannah's toes with each step. The waves' rhythmic in and out, the ever-present salty breeze, and the call of gulls hoping to find a bit of food was the background of her existence.

And Hannah loved every second of it. Her Great Aunt Caro-

21

line left her with more than an oceanside property; she left Hannah a way of life that she would never abandon.

"Aunt Hannah," Olivia's high pitched voice beckoned. "Look at what I found." She held up a piece of blue sea glass that was smooth on the edges from its time washing back and forth across the sand and rocks. "I'm adding this to my treasure box."

Hannah ran her hand over Olivia's French braid. "That box must be getting pretty full by now."

"Cal promised to make me a new box that I can lock," she announced.

"Cal is very talented." Hannah loved the cottage he'd built for her and depended on him for any and all repairs. "We'd better turn around. Samantha's on her way to pick me up and your mom is still at work so you and the dogs will be staying with Jack."

Olivia whispered in Petunia's ear, but loud enough for Hannah to hear. "Jack promised to take me to The Fishy Dish for ice cream after dinner, but I can't tell Mom."

Hannah chuckled. Jack loved to spoil Olivia with attention and ice cream. She brought out the softer side of Jack's personality.

As soon as they were in sight of Jack's house, Olivia ran ahead with Petunia trotting alongside. Nellie and Patches were already waiting at the door while Samantha and Jack chatted next to her royal blue Mini Cooper.

As Samantha twirled around, her fuchsia gauzy sundress flew out to the side. "What do you think? Will Mr. Harold the Photographer notice me?" A matching fuchsia flower was clipped to the side of Samantha's silver curls.

"Of course." Harold definitely would notice Samantha but what Hannah wondered, would it be for the reasons Samantha hoped? For a woman in her eighties, Samantha was petite, sparkly, and full of energy. But was she cut out to be a bathing suit model? Time would tell.

Petunia used her sensitive nose to examine Samantha's toes exposed through the straps of her sandals. "That tickles," she screeched and jumped. "You get to sit in the back seat, Petunia. Away from my feet." Samantha opened the door. "Hop in."

With Petunia sitting in the back seat with the seat belt strapped around her chest, Hannah in the passenger seat gazing out the window and wondering what she was headed into, and Samantha behind the wheel bopping to the rock and roll music on her radio like a teenager, they backed out of Jack's driveway toward the Paradise Inn.

With the new owner, the Inn had a new look. Hannah took in the lovely blue hydrangeas and clumps of birch trees that lined the driveway. Two small pools with water cascading over well-placed rocks had been added to each side of the front entry. It gave an elegant and relaxing impression.

Samantha jumped out of her car, raring to go. Petunia's hooves tapped on the tarred parking lot as she pranced along next to Samantha toward the entryway. And the small pools.

"Hang on to her good and tight, Samantha." Hannah imagined a disaster if Samantha wasn't paying attention and Petunia had her way.

"What?" Samantha turned her head back toward Hannah.

"The pools!"

Petunia lurched forward, ripping the leash from Samantha's grasp and settled herself in the cool water.

"Oops." Samantha reached for the leash, slipping on one of the rocks along the edge, almost tipping into the water with Petunia. She managed to catch herself and the leash but Petunia couldn't be budged.

Hannah, knowing how Petunia could be stubborn at times, had treats in her pocket. She held out a tasty molasses dog biscuit which did the trick. The only problem now was that they had a dripping wet potbelly pig.

Hannah sent Ruby a text to come out with a towel so they could get the situation under control before the growing crowd became a problem.

"Is that our dinner tonight?" one guest hollered at Hannah as he pointed to Petunia.

She clenched her fists into tight balls and glared at the man.

Samantha walked right over to him with her hands on her hips. She pointed her finger in his face. "You should be asking for an autograph. Don't you recognize Petunia the Potbelly Pig? She's here for a photoshoot."

The man's mouth fell open. "This Inn doesn't allow animals."

"Ha. It allows *working* animals. She'll have the best suite in the place." Samantha tossed her curls and marched back to Hannah. Without lowering her voice, she said, "Can you believe he even thought about eating our Petunia? What a jerk."

Ruby rushed out the front door with an armful of towels. "Thank goodness, you're finally here. Harold's nose is all bent out of shape ever since the dog-napping attempt. And once Juliette found out it was Monique, the two of them had a real hair-pulling, eye-gouging wrestling match. I have to get this under control or I'll never get the promotion I have my eye on. At least I haven't seen Monique since Harold pulled Juliette off her. She's probably in her suite licking her wounds."

Hannah rubbed her sister's back. "The first thing you have to do is calm down. As soon as Samantha gets Petunia dried off, you can show us the set-up." She nodded toward Samantha. "She wants to be in charge of Petunia in the hopes that she'll get noticed by Harold for a walk-on modeling spot."

Ruby's eyebrows shot up under her bangs. She shook her head. "I can't even think about that for now." She pulled Hannah, with Samantha and Petunia following behind, into the Paradise Inn.

"Take a deep calming breath, Ruby," Hannah told her sister. "You need to stay focused."

Ruby nodded. "Okay. I can do this." They walked through the lobby and down a hallway. "Harold has this whole wing of the Inn rented for the weekend. Besides the rooms for himself and the models, he has a suite for his inside shots plus the private pool

24

and hot tub on this wing." Ruby leaned close to Hannah's ear. "I don't know how he pulled that off, it must have cost him an arm and a leg."

They turned a corner, just as Juliette came through the door marked *pool*. Her mouth was set in a tight, thin line. Maisy, firmly tucked in her arms, whined and wiggled. Juliette dodged around Ruby, not stopping or even acknowledging her or Hannah.

"That's odd," Ruby said as she looked at the retreating figure. "She really hasn't been herself ever since the fight, but she hasn't been *ignoring* me."

A young man holding a clipboard rushed toward Ruby. "Where's Monique? Harold is livid that she's late for her time slot." He ran his fingers through his already-disheveled light brown hair. "She's not answering her phone. I pounded on her door and she never opened it. I'm dumping this on *you*, Ruby. I don't get paid enough for verbal abuse from a customer."

"I'll find her. Go back inside with Harold and try to keep him calm. Monique is a spoiled, temperamental model but I'll find her one way or another."

The young man nodded, turned around, and headed down the hallway in the same direction Juliette had disappeared.

"This is turning into one big nightmare," Ruby mumbled more to herself than to Hannah. "Samantha, you take Petunia to the room that Harold set up as his indoor studio—room one-fifteen. Hannah, you can help me search for Monique."

Samantha and Petunia disappeared down the hall.

"Who was that guy?" Hannah asked.

"Colin Simmons. He recently got hired as my event assistant but my suspicion is that he's after my event manager job so it wouldn't surprise me if he tries to undermine this whole affair to get me out of the way. I'm learning that this is a cutthroat career." Ruby started to walk down the hall. "I'll check in Monique's room first. She's probably pouting about the dog bite incident. All of this would be solved if Harold would just get rid of Monique."

Hannah stood next to her sister as Ruby pounded on Monique's closed door. Nothing. "Should I try my master key? Maybe she's hurt or something."

Hannah nodded. "Knock again and say you're going to come in."

A second round of door knocking had the same result as the first attempt. Ruby inserted her key card, the light turned green, and she pushed the door open. With the blinds drawn closed, the room was dark and stuffy.

Hannah flipped the light switch. Clothes were strewn on every available surface including the floor. "I thought this was a bathing suit shoot. Why would she have all these other clothes?"

Ruby's shoulders bobbed up and down. "She's a model is the only answer I can think of." Ruby peeked into the bathroom. "Well, she's not here. Her friend's room is next door. Apparently, Monique can't travel alone and brings Vanessa with her. Maybe *she* knows what's going on."

The two women left Monique's room and moved to the next door. Repeating the knocking got the same results. "What should I do now?" Ruby glanced at her watch. "This is going to send Harold into a meltdown."

Before Hannah could reply, the door opened. An attractive woman who could very well be, or once was, a model herself, stood looking at Ruby. "What do *you* want?"

"Sorry to bother you Vanessa, but do you know where Monique is? She's supposed to be with Harold and we can't find a trace of her."

Vanessa, dressed in a plush white terry bathrobe and with a towel wrapped around her hair, rolled her eyes. "I dared to take a half hour to myself and you've lost Monique?"

Hannah's pulse pounded at the tone and sneering look Vanessa directed at Ruby. Words fell out of her mouth before she could stop them. "I imagine your friend is quite capable of losing herself."

26

Vanessa's mouth opened and she slammed the door in their faces.

"Okay. I probably shouldn't have let that thought leave my brain," Hannah said.

"Don't worry about it. Those words were absolutely the truth but, unfortunately, it doesn't help us find her." Ruby looked up and down the hallway. "I don't know where to look next."

Petunia charged from a room at the end of the hall toward Hannah.

"Huh?"

Samantha appeared with the harness and leash dangling from her hand, but she was too far behind to catch the potbelly pig.

Petunia swerved around Hannah who managed to get a hand on her, but without her harness, there was nothing for Hannah to hang onto. Hannah, Ruby, and Samantha dashed after the fleeing pig.

As a group of people rounded a corner ahead of them, Petunia detoured through a door that happened to be propped open.

Ruby followed, straight into the room with the indoor pool and hot tub. "Pull the door closed behind you," she shouted over her shoulder. "We should be able to corner her in here."

Hannah stopped to make a strategy. Humid air engulfed her. The rectangular pool was only a few feet in front of her with the hot tub beyond. Thankfully, both were empty. Petunia stood at the shallow end of the pool with her back feet on the tiles and her front feet in the water on the first step.

As everyone slowly advanced from both sides, Petunia moved deeper and started to doggy paddle in the shallow end.

"She'll get tired soon enough," Hannah said hopefully.

Samantha stood next to Hannah while Ruby circled around the pool in case Petunia decided to try a different escape route. She crouched down and stared into the water. "Hannah?"

When Hannah saw Ruby's pale face, blinking eyes, and mouth hanging open, she rushed to Ruby's side.

Ruby pointed through the bubbles from the pool's jets. Her eyes lifted to meet Hannah's. "I recognize that red bikini and long blonde hair." Her voice came out barely over a whisper. She sat back on her heels. "Do you think she fell in?"

"That's what it looks like." Or, someone pushed her. But Hannah kept *that* thought to herself before she jumped in to try to save Monique.

CHAPTER 5

I t didn't take long before the Paradise Inn swarmed with
police. Deputy Pam Larson arrived, holding a cardboard
coffee cup. "Hannah Holiday!"

Pam's voice echoed in the tiled room as she wiggled her finger
in a gesture indicating Hannah needed to join her at the edge of
the pool. She pulled off her glasses, using the sleeve of her
uniform to wipe off the condensation.

"What happened here? You pulled this body out of the pool?"
She slid her glasses back on.

"I did, but I couldn't revive her." Hannah's head hung down.
Her whole body slumped with exhaustion. Water dripped off her
long wet braid and her clothes, making a puddle around her feet.
Someone draped a towel around her shoulders. She shivered from
the release of adrenaline, definitely not from any cold in the
steamy pool room.

"How'd she end up in the pool?" Pam sipped her coffee. Her
mouth turned down. "This is the worst coffee I've had all day, and
that says a lot."

Hannah looked at Pam. "No clue. We," Hannah indicated her

sister and Samantha with a nod of her head, "followed Petunia in here and Ruby saw the body at the bottom of the pool."

Pam smoothed some strands of her brown hair behind her ear. "You think Petunia pushed her in the pool?"

"Listen, Pam, don't put words in my mouth. I never said anyone pushed her in the pool. She was already at the bottom when we arrived."

"So, no one else was in here?" Pam swept her hand around the humid room.

"I didn't see anyone. Ruby told me that this is part of the private space that Harold Chandler had reserved for his swimsuit photoshoot but they weren't in here yet."

Pam tossed her cup into a trash can. She pulled out a notebook and jotted some notes.

Hannah couldn't help but wonder how long Monique had been at the bottom of the pool. Long enough for her to be dead but not long enough for her body to float to the surface. That should help pinpoint when she died.

"You and your friends can wait outside while we finish up in here. But don't leave the Inn," she added. "And don't forget to keep the pig with you; I might still need to question her." Pam grinned.

Hannah ignored Pam's attempt at humor or an insult. She wasn't sure which it was. Ruby slipped her arm through Hannah's. Samantha had Petunia back in her harness and held her leash as they left the pool area.

"What now?" Samantha asked.

Hannah knew that Samantha was itching to jump into an investigation, even from the sideline, since she had spent the better part of her life pretending to be a private eye. Hannah did not share that desire.

"I want to get a closer look at the crime scene." Samantha twisted her head one way then the other. "Maybe there's a back way in."

Hannah glared at Samantha. "Forget about that. Pam won't let us near the pool until every inch has been examined. Let's find Juliette. Remember how we saw her come out of the pool area when we first arrived? She might have seen something." Or done something, Hannah thought as she turned toward Ruby. "Where do you think she is?"

Ruby stopped. "You're soaking wet. I'll scrounge up some dry clothes and meet you in room one-fifteen."

Hannah suspected that Ruby had the same concern about Juliette that niggled in the back of her own brain. Juliette had been completely distracted and obviously upset when they saw her earlier as she left the pool area. Something had happened, but what?

The tapping of Petunia's hooves on the tiled floor brought Hannah back to the moment and she dashed to catch up with Samantha.

"I thought you got stuck in a daydream," Samantha said when Hannah caught up. "If we can't search around the pool, maybe we can get a jump start on information from the others who knew Monique. My guess is that room one-fifteen is where the center of all the action is at the moment."

Petunia pushed through the door and Maisy darted to greet her. The Moodle danced around the potbelly pig before lowering herself into a play bow.

Hannah's eyes scanned the room, expecting to find Juliette since Maisy was there. Harold was photographing a tall blonde model and Monique's friend, Vanessa, sat in a corner filing her nails and looking like she couldn't possibly be any more bored.

"What's going on here?" Harold's livid voice and coal black eyes fixed on Hannah. "I know you. You served us at that snack bar on the beach. What are you doing here interrupting my photoshoot?"

The model who, by her looks anyway, could have been a close relative of Monique, lowered her arms and tugged at the tiny piece of fabric that was the bottom of her bikini. "Break time, Harold?" she asked in a nasal twang.

"Not on your life, Gwen. Didn't you just take a break not that long ago? I'm not done, and with Monique still pulling one of her disappearing acts, you'll have to fill in." His attention was back on Gwen with his camera ready to begin shooting.

Gwen rolled her eyes and sighed as if she was just told she had to eat a cockroach.

"About that," Samantha interrupted.

Harold's eyes narrowed to slits. "About *what?*" He lowered his camera.

"Monique."

He relaxed slightly. "Someone found her?"

"Yes." Hannah stepped forward. "I found her. Where did you say you were about an hour ago?"

"Searching for Monique and wasting precious time getting my work done. I'm on a deadline and we're behind before we've barely even begun."

"Did you look around the pool area?"

"Of course. And I looked in her room, too, but when Monique wants to disappear she's a master at finding the best spot." His eyes moved between Hannah and Samantha. "What?"

"She found a good hiding spot, all right," Samantha said. "In the bottom of the pool."

Harold's jaw dropped. He blinked several times.

Gwen rolled her eyes again. The expression was not lost on Hannah.

Vanessa's head popped up, the nail file slipped through her fingers, and she let out an "Eek!" She jumped to her feet. "Where is she? I need to make sure she's all right."

Deputy Pam Larson entered the room. She had her notebook open. "I'm looking for a Vanessa Parkes."

"Oh, thank goodness." Vanessa rushed to Pam's side. "I just heard the news. Where is my friend? Is she going to be all right?"

Pam scowled at Hannah before she guided Vanessa to a chair. "You'd better have a seat, Ms. Parkes."

Vanessa crumpled onto the chair, her hand covering her mouth.

"Your friend's name is Monique?" Pam asked.

Vanessa nodded, her eyes big saucers.

"There was an accident and she was pulled out of the pool about a half hour ago."

Vanessa's face held a spark of hope.

Pam softened her voice. "I'm very sorry but she didn't make it."

Vanessa's head fell into her lap. Muffled sobs filled the room.

Harold approached Pam. "What do you mean...she's dead? That can't be true. She's supposed to be here modeling for me."

Hannah glanced at Gwen who had a self-satisfied smirk on her face. Apparently, there was no love lost between Monique and Gwen.

"And you are?" Pam asked Harold.

He puffed his chest out. "Harold Chandler the Third. I have this whole wing reserved for the weekend."

"Is that so? Including the pool?"

"Um...the private pool on this wing, yes."

"And when was the last time you were in that pool area?"

Harold looked at Hannah and knew he couldn't lie. "About an hour ago. I went looking for Monique." He quickly added, "But I didn't find her."

"Are you sure, Mr. Chandler the *Third*?" Pam leveled a stare at Harold that made him squirm.

"Yes." He opened his mouth to say something else but quickly shut it.

Pam put her hand on Vanessa's shoulder. "You need to come with me now, Ms. Parkes."

Vanessa nodded.

Ruby walked in as Pam and Vanessa left Harold's temporary photo studio. She handed a neatly folded pile of clothes to

Hannah. "I had extra stuff in my car if you want to get out of those wet clothes." She knelt down to pat Maisy. "Why is Maisy here and Juliette isn't?"

"In her typical irresponsible way, she dumped Maisy on me and said she wasn't feeling well. She knows the deal is that she supervises when I'm photographing. She's the one who trained the dog. It's much more difficult if she isn't here." Harold plopped onto a soft chair. He swiped both hands through his thinning hair.

"Can I take a break *now*?" Gwen whined again.

Harold waved dismissively at her. "Yeah. Go. I'll snap some photos of the dog and the pig. Maybe I'll blow off this whole swimsuit thing."

Samantha slipped out of the thin jacket she had over her sundress. "Maybe I can help." She crouched next to Petunia, slipped on the pig's sunglasses and sunhat, and smiled at Harold.

It would have been a seductive smile, thought Hannah, if Samantha was about sixty years younger. But, she had to give her credit for being comfortable with her age and image.

Harold put his index fingers and thumbs together to form a frame and looked at Samantha from several different angles. "Huh. Why not?" He handed her a big floppy hat. "Put this on and stand over there where the lights are shining."

Samantha pranced in front of the ocean backdrop with the big lights shining on her. Petunia looked up as if to ask, *what the heck are we doing?* Maisy joined them and she stood on her back legs with her front paws on Petunia's back. Harold's camera clicked and clicked as he moved around and Samantha posed in different positions. Petunia and Maisy were as cute as anything.

Hannah looked at Ruby and mouthed the words, *what now?* She cleared her throat. "Harold?"

He continued to click away.

"Aren't you concerned about your model?"

He turned toward Hannah. "Of course, but what can I do now?

34

She must have slipped into the pool. Everyone knows she couldn't swim." He turned his attention back to Samantha.

"A swimsuit model and she couldn't swim?"

"That's right. I'm surprised she was even near the pool. She had a phobia about deep water. It was becoming a problem and I told her to get over it so maybe she was working on her fear." Harold turned his back to Hannah. "Did that policewoman say if there was foul play involved?"

"No. This policewoman," Pam said on her way through the door, "never did say. What an interesting question though, Mr. Chandler. Why would it even cross your mind?"

When Harold turned back to face Pam, his face showed a deep blush under his tan. "Well...I...um, thought she either slipped or... um...something else was possible."

Pam leveled her death stare on Harold causing him to shuffle nervously. "*Something else*, as you so delicately put it, is right, Mr. Chandler. I'll need to ask you some more questions. How about you put your camera equipment away so we can get comfortable?" Pam pointed to Hannah, Ruby, and Samantha. "You can leave. I'll find you tomorrow if I have more questions. And take the pig and the dog."

Ruby scooped Maisy into her arms. She obviously wasn't going to wait to be told twice.

Hannah clipped Petunia's leash onto her halter while Samantha put her jacket back on. "Harold? Don't forget to tell Deputy Larson about Gwen and Monique's relationship. It was obvious to me that she wasn't the least bit upset about what happened to Monique."

Harold frowned.

Pam turned her attention to Hannah. "Who's Gwen?"

"One of Harold's models. I don't know any particulars except the expression I saw on her face when you said Monique was dead."

Pam pointed to a not very comfortable looking wooden chair at a small dining table. "Sit."

Harold sat.

Pam sat across from him.

Hannah heard one last question from Pam before she closed the door on her way out. "So, Harold, where were you when your girlfriend was murdered?"

Once they were in the hall, Hannah grabbed onto Ruby's arm. "Did you hear that, too? Pam asked Harold where he was when Monique was *murdered*. It wasn't an accident. He knew she couldn't swim. Do you think he had anything to do with it?"

CHAPTER 6

R uby hurried with a determined pace through the lobby and out the door.

"What's the rush?" Hannah asked as she tried to keep up while Petunia dawdled at every plant and again when they were abreast of the outside fountain. "Oh no you don't." Hannah kept the leash short and managed to keep Petunia moving toward Samantha's car.

"Meet me at my house. I'll explain what I know when we're all there." Ruby continued to her car with a wiggling and whining Maisy in her arms.

"Something must have happened when she went looking for Juliette," Hannah said to Samantha as they followed Ruby's taillights. "And it just makes no sense that Juliette abandoned Maisy with Harold unless she was in some kind of trouble."

"And now you're thinking that she's in hiding?" Samantha turned her head for a second to look at Hannah. "That *she* killed Monique?"

"That's exactly what I'm thinking." Hannah drummed her fingers on her still-wet jeans. Amid all the confusion, she hadn't found the few minutes needed to change into Ruby's dry clothes. "I hope we get some answers shortly."

Samantha parked behind Ruby's white Subaru. The house was dark with just the tiniest sliver of light peeking around the edge of her drapes. Someone was inside with some lights on. Hannah walked Petunia to her backyard pen and removed her leash and harness. "I'll bring some food out in a minute."

Petunia ambled over to her muddy corner, knelt on her front legs, and rolled. Hannah was sure she heard a long happy sigh escaping from Petunia. "At least *you* had a fun-filled adventure."

Hannah took the last of Ruby's apples, carrots, and a big zucchini from her kitchen while the murmur of voices coming from the front of the house piqued her curiosity. She hurried back out to feed Petunia, who trotted to the gate and waited patiently for her dinner. Hannah gave her a quick rub behind her ears where she was still nice and clean.

By the time Hannah joined the others, Ruby was arguing. "Juliette, if you disappear, you *will* look guilty."

As far as Hannah was concerned, the looking guilty part had already happened. She turned to Juliette. "What's going on? We saw you leaving the pool area when we arrived at the Paradise Inn."

Ruby interrupted. "Go change your clothes first, Hannah. You're still wet and I don't want you to make a big stain on my couch. I'll get some drinks and snacks while you're changing."

That was the best thing Hannah had heard for the past couple of hours. She had forgotten the dry clothes Ruby gave her in the car so she went through Ruby's closet and found comfy sweatpants and a t-shirt. Peeling off her wet clothes and slipping into soft dry ones lifted her mood immensely.

"Okay," Hannah said when she returned to the living room. "Juliette, you have some explaining to do." She sat in Ruby's wooden rocker next to the coffee table with all the food. Her stomach growled, reminding her that nothing had been sent down for way too long.

Maisy was curled on Juliette's lap, sound asleep and snoring lightly after her busy afternoon. Ruby handed Hannah a glass of wine.

Juliette's fingers rubbed Maisy's paw. Her head hung and her long hair covered part of her face. "I heard Monique and Harold having a huge argument about how she was being too much of a prima donna. He threatened to give the top spot to Gwen if she didn't shape up."

"Did Harold know you heard the conversation?" Hannah asked after a satisfying sip of wine.

"I don't know. That's the problem. I was in the exercise room next to the back entrance to the pool. Harold grabbed Monique's arm and she gasped. She told Harold, 'That's the last thing you'll do to me,' and then she laughed."

"You think Harold followed her into the pool and pushed her in?"

Juliette shrugged. "Here's the thing. I didn't give any of it too much thought at the time. I know how Harold can be. He always gets his way so I was a little surprised at Monique's words, but in light of what happened..." Her voice drifted off.

"What else, Juliette?" Hannah asked, keeping her voice soft.

Juliette finally looked at Hannah, her eyes sunken and haunted. "It wasn't until after I took the shortcut through the pool area and saw her body at the bottom of the pool when I realized that Harold was certainly capable of killing Monique." She looked at each person staring at her. "If he thought he'd get away with it and made it look like an accident."

"Why did you dump Maisy and disappear, though?" Hannah couldn't wrap her head around what Juliette said. Was she actually covering her tracks for something *she* had done to Monique?

Juliette shifted which caused Maisy to lift her head. "It's okay,"

Juliette crooned as she patted Maisy until she settled back down on her lap. "I know this all looks bad, but I guess I panicked. I wasn't sure if Harold knew I was in the exercise room and heard the argument. If I left with Maisy, he'd definitely be suspicious so, as difficult as it was, I dropped Maisy off for the photoshoot and told Harold I wasn't feeling well. He was mad but I ignored his scowl and left."

"You panicked. Why didn't you try to pull Monique out of the pool? Or at least go get help?" Hannah's mind raced through all the possibilities that might have saved Monique's life unless Juliette didn't do any of them because she already knew that Juliette was dead.

Juliette pushed stray hairs out of her face. "Like I said before, I know it looks bad. I knew Monique didn't know how to swim, so the fact that she was at the bottom of the pool just looked like *more* than an accident to me." Her shoulders rose. "That's the best answer I have."

Ruby moved next to Juliette. She gave her a hug. "We'll help you get through this. And now you have Maisy back." She also threw Hannah a glare as if to say *back off with all the questions.*

"Until Harold gives me trouble," Juliette said. She wiped a tear that leaked down her cheek.

"You'll have to tell Deputy Larson what you heard," Hannah said.

Juliette's eyes opened wide. "I can't. If I admit to being near the pool when Monique died, Harold will twist it so I'm the person who looks guilty."

"But you overheard that argument. What would *your* motive be?" Ruby asked.

"Are you kidding? They all saw the terrible fight that I had with Monique after I found out it was her that tried to steal my wittle Maisy."

"Oh, I forgot about that," Ruby answered.

"And," Juliette continued. "Monique," she spit out the name, "is the reason that Harold and I are in the middle of this messy divorce to begin with. All she had to do was shake her tiny bottom and, well, Harold couldn't help himself." Her voice raised to a fevered pitch and her tears flowed freely by the time she finished that rant.

"I see your problem," Hannah said. Actually, she saw *more* than a problem for Juliette, she saw the very real possibility that she'd committed a crime. And with the way Ruby was consoling Juliette, it wouldn't be easy to convince Ruby that her friend might be a murderer.

Before anyone figured out what to do next, Ruby's front door opened. Nellie and Patches burst through first, followed by Jack carrying a very limp and sound asleep Olivia. "I saw your car in the drive so I decided to bring her home." He looked at the women sitting in the living room. "What's going on here? Did someone die?"

Maisy jumped off Juliette's lap to greet the two dogs as if *she* was the hostess. She danced around on her hind legs. She was probably figuring out how to offer a treat and a drink, Hannah thought as she watched the interaction.

Ruby relieved Jack of his duties and carried Olivia upstairs.

Jack helped himself to the mostly untouched crackers and cheese. "So? Is someone going to tell me the news?"

"One of the models died at the Paradise Inn earlier," Hannah said in a flat voice. "I pulled her out of the pool."

Jack's hand stopped midway to his mouth, his eyebrows arched up. "An accident?"

Hannah shook her head. "No, murder."

Juliette stood. "It's late and it's time for me to leave. Tell Ruby I'll call her tomorrow." She didn't stick around for any goodbyes.

"What's *her* story? I hope I didn't say something to send her packing so quickly," Jack asked after the door closed behind Juliette.

"That's Ruby's friend, Juliette. It's a long story, but the short version is that she was in the wrong place at the wrong time," Hannah explained.

"Oh. She's a suspect. Or worse?"

"Something like that." Hannah felt the exhaustion in her body and didn't want to go into an explanation at the moment.

Ruby returned and picked up her unfinished wine. "Thanks for helping with Olivia, Jack. She mumbled something about ice cream?"

"That stinker! I told her that was our secret."

Ruby laughed. "Where's Juliette?"

"She said it was late and time for her to leave. She said she'd call you tomorrow," Hannah explained.

"Where was she going? Back to the hotel?" Ruby's voice trembled. "Why did you let her leave?"

"She's a grown woman, Ruby. Why would I stop her?" Hannah shot an annoyed look at her sister. "You're always telling me not to boss *you* around but you want me to boss your friend?"

"Jeez, Hannah." Ruby ran her hands through her hair. "I'm afraid she's going to disappear. I want to help her, not chase her away."

Hannah sat next to Ruby. Their knees touched. "You *do* think she's in trouble."

"Of course I do but I was trying to calm her down. *You* kept asking all those questions and I could tell she was about to have a panic attack."

Maisy jumped onto the couch next to Ruby. "Juliette left *you* here? I don't like this at all."

"What do you want to do now?" Hannah asked. She agreed with her sister. Juliette would never leave her beloved Maisy behind unless she was desperate.

"I'll keep Maisy here. Maybe Juliette was so distracted she forgot and will come back for her. If not, I'll wait for her to call me tomorrow like she told you."

Hannah's stomach twisted into a knot. Either Juliette was afraid for her own life or she was on the run from taking someone else's.

CHAPTER 7

Sunday started as one of those too-good-to-be-true, blue sky with a balmy breeze kind of days. A day that would be perfect if you had all the time in the world to spend on the beach with nothing more important to do than watch the waves do their endless dance.

But Hannah suspected this postcard-perfect day didn't have any leisurely wave-watching time built in for her.

Her phone buzzed with a text message before her feet even had a chance to slide from under her warm covers. With Nellie stretched out on one side of her and Patches on the other, it took her a few minutes to get untangled from their weight on the cotton blanket. Not that she had much of a desire to read the text after the problems from the night before.

When Hannah finally moved Nellie and Patches out of her way, she padded into her kitchen. A loud rap on her door made her jump. "Text messages, visitors, can't a girl enjoy a few minutes to herself in the morning?" she muttered to herself as she pulled the door open.

"Ruby is annoyed that you didn't answer her text. She asked me to come over and give you a good shake." Jack grinned and walked into Hannah's cottage. He plopped on the soft chair that faced the ocean. "She's beyond worried about Juliette and needs your support." "I can offer support but I'm afraid they both will want more than that." Hannah stood in front of her window and let the peaceful view wash over her. Not that it helped a whole lot to calm the fluttering butterflies in her stomach.

"What do you mean? Maybe you can give me the long version now."

"Juliette had a big fight with Monique after she tried to steal Maisy."

"Why on earth did she do that? And I'm not referring to the fight." Jack's face turned into a mass of wrinkles when he scrunched his eyes together. "I'd have wanted to bash her, too."

"I can only speculate on Monique's motive for attempting a dog-napping heist, but I think it could have had something to do with her romantic interest in Harold, Juliette's almost-ex-husband, and the fight Harold and Juliette are having over custody of Maisy. Maybe she wanted to stir that pot of resentment thinking it would help her gain favor with him." Hannah shrugged. "Now that I say my theory out loud, it sounds pretty ridiculous, but Monique's dog-napping attempt does give Juliette a pretty strong motive to hate her. And there was no shortage of witnesses to their fight."

Jack shook his head. "Hate maybe, but murder? Wow. Dog custody in the center of a murder? So, you think Juliette might be the murderer and you don't want to get sucked into the investigation?"

"I don't want to be in the middle of two warring married people. Given the circumstances that I know at this point, and Ruby thinks it's a possibility too, Juliette is definitely a top suspect. Or will be once Pam gets all the details."

Jack stood next to Hannah. "Consider this. If so many people are aware of that fight between Juliette and Monique, someone could try to frame Juliette as an easy scapegoat."

"That's true. And here's another interesting tidbit—it was common knowledge that Monique didn't know how to swim."

"Well, *that* just takes the cake. How ironic to have a swimsuit model who can't swim."

Hannah's phone beeped with a new text message, interrupting their conversation. She sighed. "I better tell Ruby I'm on my way before she has a meltdown. Or worse." Hannah swiped the screen of her phone. "Huh. It's not Ruby. It's a message from Meg. I need to stop at The Fishy Dish kitchen on my way to Ruby's. Coming?"

"Sure. If nothing else, I can help with Olivia again. Maybe get her to try a new flavor of ice cream today."

Hannah laughed. "You love to spoil that girl, don't you?"

"I'm trying to get to the top of her best friend list. With Cal away, I have half a chance."

"Devious. But he'll be back today and he'll probably bring a gift for Olivia."

"What could Cal possibly bring back from his fishing trip that's better than ice cream?"

Hannah shrugged. "A seashell?"

Jack scoffed and mumbled under his breath. It sounded to Hannah like Jack said that Cal didn't play fair.

While Hannah slipped her feet into her flip-flops, Nellie and Patches eagerly waited at the door with their tails banging against her legs. They knew the morning routine and they had no intention of letting Hannah miss their daily morning walk on the beach.

She sent Ruby a text that she would be over as soon as possible as they trudged down the short path to The Fishy Dish. Meg had an assortment of coffee cakes, muffins, and scones lined up on the counter. "I need someone to test my new creations. And I don't mean those four-legged critters waiting at the door." She opened a jar and fished out two big dog bones for Patches and Nellie. "That should keep them busy for the time being."

Jack lowered his face toward the pastries, closed his eyes, and inhaled deeply. "Ah. What a treat first thing in the morning."

Meg pushed him away from the food and scolded, "You can't have any since you don't seem to be able to keep a secret."

Jack's shoulders sagged and his head hung down like a chastised puppy. Meg laughed. "Okay. I can't resist that hang-dog look of yours, Jack. Just don't go blabbing around town about my new baking endeavors."

"Why the secrecy? Everything you make is delicious. If I were you, I'd shout it from the top of the gazebo on the town green so everyone knew." Jack held both hands out in a gesture of confusion.

"I don't want people to know until I'm good and ready for them to know. I'm still tweaking my recipes, and the last thing I want is for a bunch of people to show up asking for a piece of my raspberry coffee cake or a cranberry muffin or lemon pecan scone before I'm ready to offer them to our guests staying at the cottages." She put her hands on her hips. "So, do you want to test for me or get out of my kitchen?"

Hannah tried to keep the edges of her mouth from twitching into a grin as she watched her cook, and apparently, now her baker, argue with her oldest curmudgeon friend.

Jack remained silent.

"Okay. I'll take that as an understanding of my demands." She handed Hannah and Jack each a small plate. "Help yourselves, but don't just wolf anything down. Eat slowly and be honest about what you think."

Hannah took a helping of each item. She couldn't decide if Meg really wanted anything but positive feedback or not but her mouth salivated just looking at the sweet treats.

First, Hannah nibbled on the lemon pecan scone. It was light and soft, with the perfect touch of tart, but with an added crunch from the pecans. "Heavenly. Five stars for this."

Meg smiled.

Next, Hannah sampled the cranberry muffin. She let the flavors sit on the back of her tongue before she swallowed. "A little too sweet for my liking, but other than that, it's moist and tender."

Meg nodded. "That's an easy fix."

The raspberry coffee cake begged to be tasted, and the memory of yesterday's delicious treat made Hannah's stomach rumble. The crumbly streusel that wove through the cake promised satisfaction in every bite. Hannah had left what she knew was the best for last. Juicy raspberry flavor squirted in her mouth and mixed with the rich brown sugar streusel. "Ahhhh. Better than the taste I had yesterday. You've added more streusel and it's a bit moister. This one gets five plus stars for sure."

"I told you, Meg. You didn't believe me when I said your raspberry coffee cake was to die for." Jack helped himself to each pastry. After a taste of each, he dabbed at the corner of his mouth. "Perfection. You, dear Meg, have the magic touch when it comes to all things food."

Meg hugged Jack. "And you, Jack, just want to stay on my good side so I keep feeding you."

Their laughter was interrupted by Hannah's phone. "It's Ruby again. I'd better get to her house before she has a fit."

"What do you want me to do with these pastries?" Meg asked.

"Let the guests know they can have a complimentary pastry with coffee and price the rest for customers. I'm sure they'll disappear. Make sure you have plenty of coffee, too."

Hannah started for the back door but turned back and dropped a couple of scones and a few muffins in a bag. "For Ruby, so she's not too mad at me for taking so long to get there," Hannah explained on her way out the door where Nellie and Patches waited. They ran to the beach, stopped, and looked back at

Hannah as if to say *hurry up*. "I guess I'm taking the beach route," she told Jack. "We'll cut up by your house and continue on the road."

"Give me enough time to get home and make coffee. If Ruby's upset, she probably didn't bother to make any, and from what you've told me, she'll need some to go with those scones."

Hannah caught up with the two dogs and slipped off her flip-flops. They charged ahead, trying to get close to an unsuspecting gull resting on the beach, but failed. It seemed as though the gulls enjoyed teasing the dogs as much as the dogs enjoyed the chase.

As she watched the game and let her toes dig into the cool wet sand, her mind tried to grasp the details that she knew so far surrounding the murder at the Paradise Inn. The heated argument between Juliette and Monique certainly gave the impression that Juliette had a motive to want Monique out of her life. She admitted to being near the pool area before Monique died, and Hannah saw her leave the pool area at what, most likely, was the time frame surrounding the death.

Did she push Monique into the pool and rush out with Maisy clutched in her arms?

Nellie barked her frustration at a gull as it just barely lifted off out of her reach.

Jack's words about someone framing Juliette rang in her ears. Instead of focusing on Juliette, Hannah wondered who else in Monique's small circle could have snuck in and out of the pool area unnoticed. If everyone knew about Monique's fear of deep water, Harold, Gwen, and even Vanessa could be suspects if they had a motive. The last explanation could be that a random person or guest at the Paradise Inn could have pushed Monique in the pool which, unfortunately, opened up a much bigger pool of suspects.

Nellie and Patches streaked to the path through the rocks at the top of the beach which led to Jack's house. When Hannah opened his front door, the strong aroma of his rich coffee aroused her senses. Jack being Jack, and knowing Hannah's love of his blend, handed her a mug with a splash of cream swirling through the dark steamy coffee.

"You know me too well, Jack." She held the mug up. "Thanks."

"I've got the rest in this thermos. Let's get to Ruby's house and see what awaits us."

They quickly matched their strides and followed the two dogs who had figured out where the next stop was. Hannah sipped her coffee, careful not to spill any. "What do you think?"

"I think a lot, but what particular subject are you referring to?"

"You know, about getting involved to help Juliette."

"I think, Hannah, even if you don't want to, you will because you always help people. It's your nature." They walked a few more paces in silence. "And, if you don't, Ruby will never talk to you again."

Hannah knew that Jack's last comment was an exaggeration to try to lighten the difficult situation, but she also knew that his first answer was the truth.

She wouldn't be able to ignore Juliette.

CHAPTER 8

J ust as Hannah suspected, Ruby hadn't slept much. Her hair was a stringy mess and she still wore the same clothes from the night before.

"Go take a shower and put on clean clothes," Hannah said before she offered Ruby the coffee or a pastry. "Then we can talk."

Ruby dragged herself off her couch and trudged upstairs.

Olivia, on the other hand, sat on the floor with Maisy curled between her legs. "And this is my bestest friend, Theodore. You probably won't believe it, but he's old and you can talk to him if you want to. He always keeps secrets."

Maisy lifted her head to look at Olivia when Nellie and Patches approached. "Oh, your other friends are here now. You can go say hello."

Hannah let the three dogs outside, knowing that Nellie and Patches would stick around and hoping that Maisy would stay with them. "Maisy's a sweet dog, isn't she, Olivia?"

"Yeah, but Mommy said she's only visiting until Juliette gets back."

If Juliette comes back, Hannah thought. "Well, I'm sure Juliette will be happy to have you keeping Maisy such good company."

She held her hand out toward Olivia. "Come sit at the table. I brought a surprise."

Olivia's eyes zeroed in on the bag in Hannah's hand. Her eyes grew big and she smiled. "What did you bring, Aunt Hannah?"

"It's a surprise."

"Something I'll like?"

"I hope so."

Olivia climbed onto her chair and sat on her knees. Hannah opened the bag. "Do you want to reach in?"

Never one to embrace the unknown, she shook her head and curled her small fists into balls close to her chest. Hannah pulled out a muffin and offered it to Olivia.

"Oh. That looks yummy." She happily accepted the treat. "Can I have some hot chocolate with it?"

"Okay." Hannah busied herself with heating milk and adding cocoa. She dumped a spoonful into her coffee for a hot chocolate mocha twist but she was careful not to let Jack see her. He was a coffee purist.

Ruby entered looking refreshed, clean, and a bit happier. She kissed the top of Olivia's head. "What's that?"

"Aunt Hannah made me hot chocolate and gave me a muffin. She's got more in the bag."

Jack filled a mug with his coffee for Ruby and she helped herself to a scone. "Where'd these come from? Did you get up bright and early to do some baking?" She raised her eyebrows as she looked at her sister.

"Um. Yeah. You know how much I love to bake."

Before Hannah or Jack spilled Meg's secret, Ruby's front door opened. Maisy dashed into the kitchen and put her front feet on Olivia's chair. Hannah, Jack, and Ruby looked at the new arrival.

Juliette stood in the doorway and mumbled. "I...um...needed some space last night."

"Okay." Ruby said with an unmistakable edge to her tone.

"I...I'm sorry for taking off," Juliette said, her eyes looking everywhere but at the people focused on her. "I couldn't sit still and I needed to get some answers."

"Geez, Jules. I didn't sleep all night worrying about you. I was afraid I'd read about the police finding you dead somewhere." She quickly covered her mouth and looked at Olivia who, fortunately, was too busy enjoying her muffin and hot chocolate while she talked to Maisy.

"I could use some coffee if you have more." Juliette cocked her eyebrow in question. Jack drained his thermos and handed her a mug.

With her eyes closed, she sipped, sighed, and relaxed her shoulders.

Hannah offered her the bag. "Help yourself if you want something to go with your coffee."

"The muffins are delicious," Olivia said. "Can I have another one please, Aunt Hannah?"

"Um—"

"No." Ruby jumped in before Hannah had time to indulge her niece. "I think we should all sit in the other room and hear what Juliette did last night."

Olivia wrapped her arms around Maisy and half-carried and half-dragged the small Moodle into the living room. "We can sit over here with Theodore," she told Maisy.

Hannah needed to get this conversation rolling so she could get back to her business before the whole morning was lost. "Did you discover anything, Juliette?"

"I bumped into Ruby's assistant, Colin, and he had plenty to tell me."

The others leaned a bit closer to Juliette. Hannah tried to read Juliette's expression but she couldn't tell if Colin's information was good or bad for her.

"The good news is that there are several suspects." She paused. "The bad news is, according to what Colin heard, all those other suspects are throwing me right to the sharks. What am I going to do?"

Ruby, Hannah, and Jack all started talking at once. Jack's voice won. "You may not know this, but my daughter is a policewoman in town—Deputy Pam Larson? Did you talk to her yet?"

Juliette shook her head. "I wasn't around when she questioned everyone yesterday, but Colin said she's trying to track me down. Can you tell her I'm innocent?" Juliette's eyes pleaded with Jack.

"Well, Pam is an independent but fair police officer and will be methodical in her investigation. My advice is to tell her your side, sooner rather than later. Don't let her get the impression that you've disappeared because you are trying to run away from something. You know what I mean?"

She nodded.

"Before you leave to talk to Pam, did Colin say who the others are that are trying to make you look guilty?" Hannah asked.

"It's not hard to figure out that Harold was the most vocal. Of course. He's telling everyone that it has to be me because of that fight I had with Monique."

"Sometimes, the one who yells loudest is the one trying to hide his own guilt," Hannah said. "Do you know if Harold had a reason to want Monique out of his life enough to give her a nudge into the pool?"

Juliette finished her coffee but the muffin was untouched. "Ha! It wouldn't surprise me at all but I don't know any specifics. He uses people until they annoy him, and I had the impression that Monique had reached beyond the annoyance stage. But kill her?"

"Except that he had the perfect person to take the fall," Ruby pointed out. "You. He could get rid of Monique and you at the same time."

"There's more." Juliette scrunched up her mouth. "Vanessa, Monique's friend, said she saw me enter the pool area after Monique had disappeared. Of course, she didn't think to look near the pool since Monique was afraid of water, she told Colin."

"What were you doing in the pool area?" Hannah asked.

"Samantha and I saw you come out and you looked to be in a hurry." Hannah left out the part about Juliette looking distracted and panicked.

"I *was* in a hurry. I lost track of the time when I was in the exercise room and the shortest route to the room Harold set up for his photoshoot was through the pool area. I knew I was late getting Maisy there and I didn't want to upset Harold any more than possible."

Hannah didn't miss Juliette's fingers as they shredded a napkin to confetti. Her nerves were definitely on edge but was it because she knew she was in a difficult situation from being in the wrong place at the wrong time, or because she had something to hide?

"Oh, Juliette, try not to worry. The truth will come out." Ruby tried to calm her friend but everyone in the room, except possibly Olivia, knew it was hopeless advice.

"Can you tell us anything about Gwen? Is she a suspect, too?" Hannah asked.

Juliette rolled her eyes. "Well, Colin tried hard to downplay that possibility. It was painfully obvious that he's head-over-heels gaga over her. But he did let one important tidbit slip." She leaned forward from her spot on the couch and actually acted like this could be important. "He was so excited that he got the chance to ask her to have a coffee with him. Guess where he accidentally bumped into her?"

"Where?" Ruby whispered.

"Gwen sashayed through the door from the pool with a towel wrapped around her itty bitty bikini." Juliette looked from one face to another. "That sure got Colin's attention. And he knows it was during the time Monique was missing because it was almost his break time."

"Listen, Juliette. You should stay here with me until this settles down. I have space, and Olivia is already attached to Maisy." Ruby stood. "I'll fix up the guest room."

"I couldn't," Juliette said.

"You can and you will. I won't take no for an answer. Come on and I'll show you where you can put your stuff."

"Before you go upstairs," Hannah interrupted, "I'm curious about Colin."

Both Ruby and Juliette spun around.

"He dumped a lot of information on you. Why? Is he trying to protect someone, or even himself? Ruby, is there a reason why Colin might have pushed Monique into the pool? He had to have been in the area to know all the facts about other people."

"Huh." Ruby nodded her head. "I never considered him but I suppose it's possible. If he's infatuated with Gwen, like Juliette said, he might think that if he got rid of Monique, Gwen would be the top model. And maybe she'd want to reward him for helping her."

"And what about your job, Ruby? You told me you suspected that he was after your position. If something horrible like this happened on *your* watch, it would help Colin, right?"

Ruby covered her mouth with her hand. "You're right, but it seems too extreme."

"At any rate, be careful what you tell him. And keep your ears open when you go back to work. Any little detail could be a link to putting the puzzle together."

Hannah suspected that whoever pushed Monique into the pool had an extremely twisted motive.

CHAPTER 9

Hannah returned to her office, located in the front half of Cottage One, or, more recently christened, *Run on Inn*. Cal had carved the new name on a piece of driftwood which hung next to the door.

"It's about time you got back here," Samantha scolded. "Ever since I moved into the other half of this cottage and offered to help out, it doesn't mean I want to be cooped up in the office missing all the excitement. What's going on?"

"Juliette is back at Ruby's house and will be staying there for a while. Other than that, there's nothing new." Hannah sat in the chair facing her Great Aunt Caroline's big old oak desk.

Samantha smiled as her fingers beat a rhythm on the desk. "Aren't you going to ask if there are any new guests?" She raised one eyebrow, giving Hannah a lopsided challenge.

"You'd better not take up poker since I can see all over your face that you have something you're bursting to tell me. Let me guess. Someone involved with the murder is staying here?"

"Well..." Both of Samantha's hands slapped on the desk. "We had a last-minute cancellation and guess who called looking for an accommodation?"

Hannah crunched up her mouth. "Who?"

"Monique's friend. Remember Vanessa? She said she couldn't spend one more minute at the Paradise Inn with all the bad memories, but she's not allowed to leave town."

"Is she a suspect?" Hannah was shocked at the thought of Monique's friend being involved in the murder other than feeling guilty for not being with Monique to protect her.

"I suppose it's a formality since everyone involved with the photoshoot has to be a potential suspect until alibis are verified. Pam told her to stay and she's *not* happy about it, but," Samantha's eyes gleamed, "with her here, right under our noses, we'll be able to keep an eye on her and question her for more backstory on all the players."

This comment gave Hannah pause. She was slightly nervous at Samantha's obvious excitement about the prospect of getting involved with some sleuthing. She would have to keep her eyes on Samantha to make sure *she* didn't get herself into any trouble. Before Friday night, Hannah's weekend had held such promise of being nice and quiet but, instead, it had turned into drama and chaos at every corner.

"Did you hear me, Hannah?"

Samantha had her hand on the door, ready to leave the office.

"I'm going to get Cottage Four ready for her. Oh, yea, it's called *Something's Fishy* now. What an appropriate name. Her huge grin confirmed Hannah's fears.

"Wait a minute, Samantha." Hannah stood and stopped the door from swinging closed. "What exactly do you plan to do? Pam won't like it if you start poking around and asking her suspects a lot of questions."

"Hannah, my dear, Officer Pam Larson can't stop me from having a friendly conversation. I suspect that poor Vanessa will be needing a shoulder to cry on, and who better than little old grandmotherly Samantha Featherstone to the rescue? I'll bet my grannie panties that Vanessa has a few theories about who had it in for her friend." Samantha winked.

Hannah couldn't argue with that observation and, in the long run, as long as the murder got solved, did it really matter where the information came from? A quiet knock on the door brought Hannah's attention back to the moment.

Vanessa stumbled through the door on her high heel sandals, weighted down with two over-stuffed, somewhat shabby, canvas bags. She dropped the bags with a thud and let herself sink into the chair next to the door. "Is this *Holiday Hideaway?* I called earlier."

"You're in the right place." Hannah touched Vanessa's shoulder, recognizing her from yesterday. "I'm sorry about your friend."

Vanessa looked up at Hannah, her blotchy face showing through a lousy makeup cover attempt. "Oh, aren't you the one who found...who pulled..." Her words faded away as her hands covered her face.

"Yes. I'm Hannah Holiday, the owner of the cottages. We're getting your cottage ready so, if you want, you can wait in here or go to the snack bar for coffee. You might find it restful to sit at one of the tables and look at the ocean view."

"Okay." Vanessa's voice registered barely above a whisper. "Can I leave my bags in here? They're kind of heavy to drag back and forth."

"Sure. Come on, I'll walk you over."

As Vanessa's heels sank in the sand, Hannah held her elbow to help her keep her balance. Why anyone would wear such uncomfortable and impractical footwear was beyond her imagination. She loved her flip-flops and wouldn't trade them for anything. Except bare feet whenever possible.

"I can't even believe this all isn't some sort of nightmare," Vanessa said. "I let Monique out of my sight for a minute and this terrible, terrible..." She shook her head. "She always was the type to make the wrong choices but I never thought something like this would happen." She stopped suddenly and looked into Hannah's eyes. "Will that policewoman find the killer? Someone needs to pay for this."

Hannah was a bit taken aback at the hostility in Vanessa's voice. "Officer Pam Larson is very thorough. She'll get to the bottom of whatever happened." Hannah wanted to reassure Vanessa even though Pam sometimes followed the wrong trail.

"I told her that Gwen was trouble from the moment I met her. All she cared about was taking as many breaks as possible and flirting with Harold. She had her eye on him and tried to undermine Monique at every turn." Vanessa swiped her cheek with the back of her hand.

Hannah tapped Vanessa's arm to get her moving again. It didn't work.

"You know what I think?" Vanessa asked, her eyes square on Hannah's again.

Hannah shook her head.

"I think Gwen followed Monique and pushed her in the pool. *She* knew Monique couldn't swim."

Samantha pushed in between Hannah and Vanessa. "Vanessa Parkes? I talked to you on the phone. Your cottage is ready."

"I was just taking Vanessa to The Fishy Dish for some coffee. How about you join us?" Hannah glared at Samantha. For someone who thought of herself as a private investigator, she certainly needed to work on her timing.

"I can do that." Samantha took Vanessa's arm. "I heard the phone ringing as I rushed by the office. Maybe you'd better see what that was about." Samantha flicked her head back toward the office.

What the heck, Hannah thought as Samantha led Vanessa toward The Fishy Dish. What was she trying to prove? Did she think Vanessa would be her big chance to finally find the clues to solve a murder? Samantha was going to be a bigger problem for Hannah than she originally expected if she jumped into her sleuthing persona with both feet and no thought.

Hannah watched as Samantha wrapped her arm through Vanessa's and helped her through the sand to one of the picnic tables. Samantha was busy yacking to Vanessa but the words were blown away in the wind.

Maybe Samantha knew what she was doing. That was what Hannah hoped, anyway.

She dashed into her office to try to catch the ringing phone. "Holiday Hideaway. How can I help you?"

"This is Harold Chandler the Third. I came to your snack bar for lunch the other day. I'm sure you remember who I am. I need a cottage for a few days."

No hello. No please. This guy expected to get exactly what he wanted. It was an interesting dilemma, Hannah thought. Two of the main suspects staying right under her nose.

"Well—"

"For myself and another cottage for my friend," he added.

His friend? Could that be for Gwen? That would bring all the suspects to her doorstep and Juliette just down the road. "Well, Mr. Chandler—"

"The Third," he interrupted.

"Yes, well, I will have *one* cottage available at three this afternoon, but unfortunately, the others are all booked."

"That will have to do. The police won't let me use the wing I reserved at the Paradise Inn and I can't stand where I've been moved to. No privacy." Hannah heard a long sigh through the phone. "I'm hoping to get some beach shots at least, so this weekend isn't a total waste of my time."

"The beach is right out the cottage door."

"Oh, and is that lady with the pig around? I'd love to do some more photos of that pair. And Maisy if Juliette ever shows up. *She's* got some explaining to do. Especially to the police." A chuckle hit Hannah's ear.

Hannah was surprised that Harold was venting to her as if they had some kind of actual history together after only meeting twice. "The room will be ready for you at three, Mr. Chandler." Hannah heard the phone click. Maybe he didn't like it that she forgot to add *the Third* after his name. She didn't forget, she refused to feed his ego.

Hannah headed to The Fishy Dish to see if she had any fires to put out in the kitchen. Meg easily got her nose bent out of shape if Hannah got distracted taking care of other business. She bumped into Samantha carrying a tray with coffee and one of Meg's delicious new pastry creations out of the snack bar. "Is Vanessa settled into her cottage yet?"

"She decided to have coffee and something to eat first. The poor woman doesn't know if she's coming or going and you wouldn't believe all the stories pouring out, one after the other. She can't get them out fast enough."

"Oh? About Monique?"

"Monique, Harold, Gwen, you name it. Between chaperoning her friend at these photoshoots and making sure no one took advantage of Monique, to having nothing to do now, I don't know, Hannah. I think she might have a nervous breakdown."

"She's probably in shock."

"Definitely." Samantha moved away from Hannah. "And there's some serious anger ready to lash out at whoever did this to Monique. I'll get this to her and help serve the other customers."

"Keep an eye on Vanessa. We've got two new guests arriving this afternoon."

Samantha stopped and turned back to face Hannah.

"Harold Chandler and Gwen." Hannah raised her eyebrows.

Samantha's eyes widened and the corners of her lips twitched up. "This is getting more and more curious, don't you think?"

"Uh-huh. All I need is for Pam to show up and accuse me of harboring a killer."

"Ha! You might be, but if we put our heads together, maybe we can flush him out for her."

"Him?" Hannah asked.

"Or her." Samantha had a light step and side-to-side sway as she brought the coffee and pastry to Vanessa's table.

CHAPTER 10

Hannah heard whistling when she finally entered the kitchen. Meg couldn't follow a tune if her life depended on it, but if she was whistling, it meant she was in a good mood.

"The couple staying in Cottage Three that's leaving today?" Meg said to Hannah as she entered the kitchen. "They *loved* my raspberry coffee cake. Couldn't stop singing its praises. As a matter of fact, after the complimentary piece with their coffee, they bought the rest to bring home, plus some scones and muffins."

"Offering a free sample is the best advertising." Hannah lifted the cover on the tray of pastries. "Everything is gone?"

"The last one went out with Samantha for that needy blonde. I'll make a double batch for tomorrow." Meg leaned on the counter with her wooden spoon tapping a rhythm on the edge of her mixing bowl. "I've got a favor to ask."

This wasn't the self-sufficient, never needed anyone else's help Meg that Hannah met when she first moved to Hooks Harbor. Something smelled fishy about the request. "What kind of favor?"

Meg's lower lip puffed out. "After all I've done for you, you are questioning my need? This is hard enough, me asking for help, without you giving me that look like you just bit into a slice of lemon."

Hannah held up her hands to ward off Meg's rant. "I'll help, no worries, but can't you give me a hint about what I'm agreeing to?"

Meg rubbed her jaw. "My twin brother, Michael?"

Hannah nodded. Michael owned the Pub and Pool Hall, a hangout for the locals and any out-of-towners that managed to wander down the pothole-filled dirt road that ended at his establishment. He did serve excellent pizza and a wide variety of beer which more than made up for the lack of a cozy ambiance. Or any ambiance for that matter.

"He bought a cottage and wants your opinion on redecorating. You know, since you did such a great job with the cottages. He wants a casual but cozy feel. Will you help?"

"Of course."

"Great. I'll pick you up around four." Meg pointed her wooden spoon at Hannah. "And no faces or comments about my truck. It hasn't let me down yet."

"*Yet* being the key word. How about I drive this time?" Hannah hated Meg's rust bucket with springs poking through the seats and more squeaks and rattles than in a bucket of noisy dog toys.

"No. I'll pick you up. I've got a couple of things to bring to the new place." Meg returned her attention to her chowder and her whistling letting Hannah know that the conversation was over. If she was lucky, the cottage wasn't too far away and the torture of riding in Meg's truck would be short.

Hannah pushed through the kitchen door to help a group of lunch customers. Everyone wanted the fried fish platter and they'd be outside at one of the tables.

The rush was on.

Hannah gave the order to Meg and was relieved to see Samantha arriving to help with the lunch crowd. "Is Vanessa checked into her room?"

"Yes. She said she's going to take a nap so I don't think we'll see her for the rest of the afternoon."

"Good. That will put off any potential confrontation with Harold and Gwen when they arrive. It seems I'll be spending all my time trying to avoid being in the middle of several dysfunctional relationships." The very last place she wanted to be at any time.

"Don't turn around now," Samantha said as she looked over Hannah's shoulder. "Harold and Gwen just got out of his car. The photography business must be doing well for him if that fancy bright red Alpha Romeo is an indication of his income."

"Or debt," Hannah said as she tried to reposition herself to get a glimpse of what was heading her way. From the corner of her eye, she could see Harold standing next to the driver's door, swiveling his head in all directions. "Is he hoping for a valet service here?"

"I'll offer to help with his bags. That should make him feel about this high." Samantha put her thumb and forefinger about a quarter inch apart. "He's got almost half a foot on me and at least seventy pounds. Do you think he'll actually let *me* carry his bags?"

"Probably. The guy has an ego bigger than this ocean from the little bit I've interacted with him. Besides, you're probably stronger than he is. His body is a far cry from the sleek toned bodies that his models have."

Samantha headed toward the parking lot. She waved to Harold. "Yoo-hoo, Harold. Do you need some help?"

He opened the back door and pointed inside. Hannah couldn't hear their conversation but Samantha reached inside and slid out a huge suitcase that almost ripped her arm from its socket when it slammed to the ground. Harold was already on his way to the office with Gwen tiptoeing behind. Hannah shook her head. Gwen balanced on one foot to shake sand from her other sandal after each step. It was a hopeless endeavor, of course.

Hannah waited for Harold to disappear inside the office. Let him wait, she thought. His room wasn't ready for several hours anyway. Did he think she'd magically find another cottage just because *he* needed one? She helped Samantha with the suitcase instead, wheeling it through the sand and parking it outside the office.

"There you are." He stood on the porch, looking down at Hannah. "No one is in the office," Harold stated as if he had just announced an amazing and unbelievable fact.

Hannah bit her tongue, stopping a rude comment from slipping out that would have been inappropriate to say to her guest. Instead, she tried for congenial with an overtone of helpful. "I explained over the phone that your cottage wouldn't be ready until three. You can leave your suitcase here if you'd like. Our snack bar is open and, of course, the beach," Hannah waved her hand to include the incredible view, "is always open."

"Harold." Gwen's nasally, whiney, drawn out word must not have endeared her to Harold. Hannah saw his jaw muscles tighten. "I've got sand stuck in between my toes."

"It's the *beach*, Gwen. Of *course* you'll have sand between your toes and probably other places too, if you're not careful. Get your bikini on, and I'll use this time to get some photos. The light is good, at least."

"Change? Where?" Gwen glanced back into the office. "And I'm *hungry*."

Hannah pointed toward The Fishy Dish. "You can use the bathroom inside the snack bar to change."

"I'll order food and meet you at one of the tables. Don't tie up the bathroom all afternoon."

Gwen stayed rooted to the spot on the porch. "I'll have to open my suitcase to find my bikini." She stared at the enormous suitcase as if she expected it to jump up next to her like an obedient puppy.

Hannah started to walk away and leave Gwen to solve her own problem but, instead, she decided to use the opportunity for some information gathering. "Gwen, it must be difficult for you to leave the Paradise Inn. You don't seem to be accustomed to this…ah… sandy environment."

"Oh, I'm so glad you understand. I loved Harold's indoor studio at the Paradise Inn. And the pool was simply divine. No sand…or bugs." She swatted at something that buzzed around her face. "I wouldn't even be here if it wasn't for that bossy police-woman telling us we couldn't leave town."

Hannah heaved the suitcase next to Gwen and gritted her teeth at the lie she was about to say. "I *know* how you must feel. Were you and Monique close? Did working together make you feel like, you know…you had a sort of comradery with her?"

"Are you kidding me? Monique had an agenda and it didn't include *me* hanging around Harold. She had her claws in him so far, he didn't have a chance. It was all, 'How's this, Harold?', and, 'Does my skin sparkle enough, Harold?'" Gwen's voice took on a fake high-pitched tone. "At least now, with Monique out of the way, I might get more exposure from this photoshoot."

"*Really.*" Hannah couldn't believe what she was hearing. Since when did *murder* equal *out of the way*? Was Gwen so dumb she didn't even know she just admitted to having a motive to kill her rival with talk like that? Or was she playing an act to make others think she would never expose herself if she was the killer?

Gwen lowered her voice as she rummaged through her suit-case. "Ya know what I think?"

Hannah couldn't imagine what Gwen was thinking about anything. She blinked and waited.

"When I went on my break about a half hour before Monique was found at the bottom of the pool, I saw Harold near the back entrance to the pool area. I think Monique drove Harold crazy with all her demands and in a fit of anger, he tripped her as she walked near the pool." Gwen wiped her hands. "Problem solved."

"Wasn't Monique his girlfriend?"

"That's what *she* thought, but Harold was definitely flirting with me behind her back."

"There's something I can't figure out," Hannah said. "Why would Monique even go near the pool if she didn't know how to swim and was scared of deep water?"

"She told me she was working on that. She said that Harold insisted she get over her phobia. Someone was helping her. She wouldn't have gone near the pool by herself." Gwen shrugged. "How can you be a swimsuit model and not go in the water some of the time? I think the best shots are when my skin is all shimmery from the water."

"Gwen!"

"Oops. I'd better get over to Harold. He *hates* to be kept waiting." Monique held two tiny bits of fabric that barely passed for a bikini as she carefully picked her way through the sand.

With everyone who had a motive and an opportunity to be the killer and each one pointing a finger at someone else, Hannah couldn't help but be more than curious to find out how Monique ended up in the pool.

Did Harold give her a little nudge as Gwen suggested? Did Juliette shove her in to get rid of the dog-napper? How about Colin trying to help Gwen become the number one model? Which left Vanessa looking for revenge for her friend's killer.

And all the players were about to clash under Hannah's nose. Someone was bound to say more than they should.

Keeping her eyes and ears open became a necessity now, or another body might turn up.

CHAPTER 11

M eg, true to her word, knocked on Hannah's cottage, *Slo N'
EZ*, at four on the dot.

"Be right with you," Hannah called from her bedroom. Her
head was partly under her bed while she searched for the mate to
the one flip-flop on her foot. Somehow it had rested against the
wall, along with the dust bunnies. With a grunt and a stretch, her
fingers managed to wrap around one of the thongs and slide
it out.

With both flip-flops in place, Hannah found Meg sitting on the
floor while Nellie licked her cheek and Patches plopped down
between her legs. "These two give me a better greeting than
anyone else in my life. Let's bring them along."

Hannah grabbed two leashes and wrapped the arms of her
cotton sweater around her waist. She closed and locked the door.

"Does Michael have any idea what he wants to do with his
cottage redecorating? Or do I get to have free reign?" Hannah
asked on the way to Meg's truck.

"The cottage came with some stuff left by the previous owner.
My guess is a few additions here and there will suit him just fine."

The dogs jumped into the back seat and Hannah carefully

found a safe, spring-free spot on the front seat. The door creaked and squeaked as she yanked hard, finally winning the tug-of-war to close the door.

"What made Michael decide to buy a cottage?"

Meg shrugged. "An investment, I guess."

Hannah was surprised when Meg turned into a driveway after only about ten minutes. "This is it."

A small, cedar-shingled cottage aged to a silvery grey was almost hidden by trees and blueberry bushes. A sliver of ocean was visible beyond the tidy structure.

"Ocean front? How'd Michael ever afford this?" Hannah asked. She knew the value of anything with ocean frontage, and it didn't come cheap.

"I *thought* you'd be surprised. That Pub and Pool Hall of his is a gold mine and no one suspects how much money he's been stashing away over the years. Plus, he really doesn't spend much so when he found this deal, he figured it was as good a place as any to put his money."

"Wow!" Hannah sat in the truck, waiting to get over the shock of Michael's wealth. "Wow," she repeated.

Meg let the dogs out. "Come on. The view out front is spectacular."

The two dogs raced toward the water. Hannah jogged to catch up. White rocks sloped to the cold ocean, creating a buffer between the deck on the front of the cottage and the water's edge.

"This is so much more private than my ocean front beach," Hannah said. "Michael found a gem."

"And you haven't seen the inside yet," Meg answered. She opened the door from the deck into a bright living room.

Hannah's jaw dropped. "You tricked me, Meg Holmes." Nellie squeezed past Hannah's legs to greet the person resting in a recliner that faced the ocean view.

"Hello, Hannah. Meg only did what I asked."

After a momentary muscle-freeze, Hannah remembered how

to make her legs work and she moved toward the silver-haired person. She leaned over the recliner, embracing her Great Aunt Caroline. Caroline's long fingers stroked her hair.

"I know it's risky but I had to see you." She held Hannah's arms and studied her face. "Jack has been acting odd lately."

"What do you mean?"

"He's avoiding me; not returning my calls. I'm concerned. Have you noticed anything?"

Hannah shook her head. "No."

"Of course not. You see him every day and he wouldn't want you to worry if something was going on. Watch him more carefully, okay?"

"Of course." Great, one more worry on Hannah's plate. She looked around the completely furnished living room. "Michael has good taste and I have to say, I'm relieved he actually doesn't need any help from me to decorate this place."

Meg shrugged. "It was all I could come up with when you grilled me on the favor I needed from you. It worked."

Hannah pulled a chair closer to Caroline. "How have you been?"

Caroline flicked her bony wrist. "I'm fine." She grinned. "For a dead person."

She leaned back, the expression on her face telling Hannah that something wasn't fine. "Can you keep a close eye on Jack? Maybe find him a nice quiet job in your office, with Olivia as a responsibility?"

Hannah considered Caroline's request. "I'm not sure a nice quiet job exists at my office at the moment."

"Oh?"

"Maybe you didn't hear about the murder at the Paradise Inn."

"I did, but how does that affect you?"

Hannah laid out the short version surrounding the murder. She explained that two cottages were rented to suspects and another one was staying down the road with Ruby. "I see lots of drama ahead as these people bump into each other. They've already pointed fingers at each other and it's not going to be pretty."

Meg carried a tray into the living room with three glasses of iced tea and a bowl of nuts. "This is all I could scrounge up."

"What about Jack coming here with Olivia?" Hannah asked. "It's private enough and you could put your worries about him to rest." She had trouble figuring out how she would keep an eye on all the suspects, run her business, *and* mother Jack, who would no doubt not enjoy the extra attention.

"No. I can't risk having Olivia talk about the old lady at the cottage. People would wonder who she's talking about. I'm already taking a big risk by being here. Besides, since he's avoiding me, he probably wouldn't agree to come."

"So, you'll be living here?"

"For a bit," Caroline said. She sipped the iced tea. "I was missing my ocean view so I convinced Meg to let me enjoy this scenery and ocean air for a week or two."

"Michael won't come out here. It's really an investment for him and he told me to take care of the place." Meg scrunched her mouth and twisted her hands up. "What's a girl to do?" She laughed. "Not a bad responsibility and if he does show up, I'll tell him I let a friend in."

Nellie rested her head on Caroline's lap. The old woman stroked the silky fur. "You need to take care of Jack for a while, okay Nellie?"

Nellie's tail thumped on the floor. "She's overprotective of Olivia so it should be easy to get her to stay with Jack when he's helping with her," Hannah said.

"Tell me more about this murder." Caroline let her head relax against the back of the recliner and she closed her eyes. "I promise I won't fall asleep."

"There's not too much more to tell. Juliette, Ruby's friend, is going through a messy divorce and her dog, Maisy, is caught in the middle. Harold has a photography business—"

Caroline's eyes popped open. "Are you talking about Harold Chandler III?"

"Yes, that would be the almost-ex-husband. Do you know him?"

"He and a beautiful model stayed at the cottages a few years ago, I would say it was six years ago. He was shooting a swimsuit calendar." Caroline put her finger to her lips. "I think the model's name was Juliette."

"Juliette is Ruby's friend. They must be the couple that you met, but they got married at some point after you met them and now they're splitting up," Hannah explained to Caroline.

"Look into their background. I have a vague memory that one of the models left suddenly. I don't remember the details. How long has Ruby known Juliette?"

"A year or two maybe. I'm really not sure and I have no idea how they met. I'll have to do some digging."

"Be careful. If my memory is right about them, you could be jumping into a hornet's nest."

"Harold definitely has an ego the size of the ocean, but Juliette struck me as a decent person."

"I bet he's never wrong and it's always someone else's fault."

Hannah chuckled. Caroline was correct. "The drama escalated when Monique tried to kidnap Juliette's dog, Maisy. I wonder if Harold told her to do it to make Juliette look irresponsible but whatever the motivation was, Monique mucked it all up and the dog bit her. If Harold *is* the killer, he had to get rid of Monique before she exposed his stupid plan. I'm sure the judge wouldn't have looked favorably on Harold for a stunt like that, and Juliette would have gotten custody of Maisy."

"He killed her because of a dog custody battle?" Meg asked.

"Maybe. *If* he killed her," Hannah corrected.

"The guy is a definite whack-a-doo, if that's the case. I have an idea," Meg said with a sly grin on her face. "He has ordered the fried fish platter twice now, maybe I should sprinkle something extra on his next order."

"What are you suggesting, Meg?"

"A little arsenic to clean up the gene pool?" Meg laughed. "Oh Hannah, don't look so worried. I'm only kidding. Although the *idea* is quite tempting."

"I'll give you that. Here's the rest of the story that puts Ruby's friend smack at the head of the suspect list. Juliette had a big fight with Monique about the dog-napping attempt and there were plenty of witnesses." Hannah held up her finger before Caroline or Meg could interrupt. "And, she was near the pool area at the Inn where Monique's body was found while Harold and Monique argued. If Harold knew that Juliette was close to the murder scene, it made it easy for him to implicate her."

"A convenient set of circumstances for Mr. Harold Chandler III," Meg said.

"But maybe it was an accident; Monique slid on a wet tile and fell in the pool," Caroline suggested.

"Monique didn't know how to swim and had a phobia of deep water, according to what another model told me. Her phobia was no secret."

"Somehow, you have to figure out who was with Monique when she went near the pool. Before someone else who might know something disappears," Caroline said. "I'm starting to think that he might have been behind that other model's quick disappearance all those years ago."

"That will be easier said than done," Hannah muttered more to herself than to the two women looking at her. And now the stakes were higher if another murder could be a possibility.

CHAPTER 12

By the time the rich coffee aroma seeped into Hannah's barely-awake brain, her first reaction was, *this is exactly what I need.*

Her second reaction made the hair on her neck stand up at the thought of an intruder in her cottage.

Her third reaction put a smile on her face when she saw that both Nellie and Patches stood at her bedroom door, wagging their tails happily.

She let her muscles relax as she waited for what she expected to arrive momentarily.

She wasn't disappointed.

Cal quietly pushed her door a bit and peeked through the opening. "Are you awake?" He tried to pat each dog with his free hand as the tray wobbled while he balanced it with his other hand. "Ready for coffee?"

"Is that all you have?" Hannah kept her gaze on Cal's blue eyes that always made her heart beat faster than normal and his grin that warmed that beating heart.

"Well," Cal pushed through the door and sat at the edge of her bed, "I've got two dog bones, a sprig of wild aster I found blooming on my way over, and—"

Hannah tried to kick him through the blankets but only managed to get Cal laughing. "If you can manage to drag yourself out of bed, I'll cook you up a couple of eggs in a hole. It's one of my breakfast specialties."

"I think it's your *only* breakfast specialty but I'm not complaining. Better to have one perfected item than many mediocre ones."

Cal forced his lips into a frown before he couldn't hold back any longer and he burst out laughing. "I'll take that as a compliment." He threw a dog bone to each dog and handed Hannah her coffee. "I'll have your eggs cooked to perfection by the time you join me in your kitchen."

"Before you go, how was your fishing trip?" Hannah sipped the coffee and closed her eyes for a couple of seconds to be better able to focus on the deliciousness.

"Not bad but I'm glad to be back." He winked and walked away, pausing at the door so Hannah got a good look at his trim back side.

Not bad, she said to herself. She was glad Cal was back, too.

Butter sizzled in her cast iron pan and Cal dropped the bread in, cut out a hole for the egg, and moved the hole to the side as Hannah leaned against the counter and watched him work.

"There was some drama Saturday at the Paradise Inn. Did you hear about it?" she asked as casually as possible.

Cal's eyebrows shot up as he flipped the bread over and cracked an egg into each bread hole. "Drama? When I fish I avoid the news."

"Oh. A swimsuit model, Monique Monroe, drowned in the pool."

"And? I've got a sinking feeling that there's more to this story. A lot more."

Hannah settled onto one of the chairs at her small kitchen table. "Ruby's friend, Juliette, is up to her eyeballs as a suspect."

"And?" The expression on Cal's face let Hannah know that he didn't like where this conversation was headed.

"Ruby and Juliette expect me to help get her out of the mess. And protect her dog from her almost-ex-husband, who I think could be the murderer."

Hannah saw Cal's shoulders rise and lower with a big intake of air. He didn't say anything. At first. "You can say no, Hannah. You can say this is a matter for the police." He slid the eggs onto a plate.

"Two of the suspects are renting one of the cottages—Harold, Juliette's almost-ex and his other model, Gwen. Plus, the victim's friend, Vanessa, is here, too, so I plan to keep my distance but also keep an eye on any interactions. Who knows, someone might say or do something that helps to find the killer. I can let Pam know if I see something."

Cal lifted his eyes to look directly at Hannah. An edge crept into his voice. "Or someone might do something, *like kill again*. What makes you think that there isn't more at stake than what meets the eye?"

Hannah popped one of the fried bread holes into her mouth. Partly to avoid answering immediately and partly because the crispy circle was actually her favorite part of an egg in a hole. She swallowed and tapped the end of her fork on the table. "Here's the thing, Cal. I can at least ask a few questions, you know, as the interested business owner. I'm a good listener, and the model, Gwen, loves to run her mouth. Vanessa, the victim's friend, might have some insight into Harold's behavior since she's been following Monique around through these photoshoots and Monique fancied herself to be Harold's girlfriend."

"I know you won't be able to ignore what seems to have landed on your doorstep, but, please, Hannah." Cal's eyes pleaded with her. "Be *extra* careful. A killer is on the loose and will not want you or anyone else to figure out what he or she did. And, you said that Juliette is up to her eyeballs as a suspect. Don't let her friendship with your sister sway your judgement."

And her dog, Maisy, Hannah thought. Maisy was in the middle of a mess which was no fault of hers. "Juliette is a woman scorned. She had a fight with the victim and she was near the scene of the crime. I know all that and will be careful, but the others have motives and no alibis so far."

Cal reached across the table with his fork and stole the other fried bread circle. "You're letting my hard work get cold."

Hannah tried to grab the fork but Cal was too fast and he popped the bread in his mouth.

"Hey, that's the best part!"

"You'd better get busy on the rest of that breakfast or I'll take care of it, too. I'm starting to feel kind of hungry."

"Get another plate. I'll share." Hannah relaxed at the change of conversation and tenseness in the room. Cal said what he felt he had to get off his chest and then moved on, which was fine with Hannah.

Cal put a plate close to Hannah's. She slid the second egg in a hole onto his plate. "You'll have to come down to The Fishy Dish with me to sample Meg's latest creations."

"Oh? You only shared so you could leave room for something better?" Cal put on a pouty, hurt face. "Or are you really trying to let me know that my cooking isn't up to your standards?"

"No, I *shared* so I wouldn't have to stab your hand if you tried to steal *more* of my breakfast." She smiled. "Thanks for being my sounding board and helping me keep an open mind."

"Fair enough." He finished the egg in a hole in about three bites. "What is Meg creating now?"

"You'll have to wait and see. But I guarantee that you won't be disappointed." Hannah cleaned the two plates and silverware. "I'll be back in a jiffy."

"I'll wait on the porch with the dogs," Cal said.

Hannah found her comfy plaid Bermuda shorts and her *I'd*

rather be a Mermaid t-shirt. She ran her comb through her hair and slipped her feet into her flip-flops on her way out the door.

Cal sat comfortably with his long tanned legs resting on the porch railing. Nellie sat on one side with her head on his lap and Patches lay at the top of the steps. "I'm thinking," Cal said as Hannah stopped next to him, "since there's no stopping you from doing some snooping, I'd like to help."

"Really?" The shock to Hannah's system forced her to grab hold of the doorframe.

"Yeah, really. I'm a good listener and I might be able to get that model to loosen her tongue if I invite her to my boat for a drink. What do you think about that idea?" Cal looked up at Hannah, his face a study of innocence.

"It's a *great* idea. I'll bring her over." Hannah kept her face serious as she called out what she assumed was Cal's bluff to make her jealous.

"Ah...it might go better if you aren't there, actually."

Hannah shook her head. "I don't agree. After what happened to Monique, any sensible girl wouldn't go alone to a boat with someone she doesn't know." Hannah was impressed with her quick thinking of what actually sounded like a practical argument. "You know, the whole water thing? Monique drowned in a pool and your boat is sitting on a much bigger body of water. I'll bring the pizza to go with the beer."

"She might say no anyway." Cal stuttered through a lame excuse. He pushed himself out of his chair.

Hannah laughed. "You were only trying to make me jealous, weren't you? Well, I actually think it's a great idea if Gwen agrees to go. After I saw how she tried to tip toe to the office to avoid getting sand in her open toed sandals, she'll probably jump at any excuse to leave the cottage. She's definitely not a nature type of girl."

"I don't know about you, Hannah Holiday. You read my plan like a smelly piece of old fish and turned it into a tasty chowder."

He stood and draped his arm over her shoulders. "You weren't even a tiny bit jealous?"

"For about a half second. Gwen is *so* not your type."

"And you are?" He turned his head to get a look at Hannah's face.

Hannah smiled and put her arm around his waist. "Uh-huh."

CHAPTER 13

Meg was bent over, sliding a tray from the oven when Hannah and Cal walked into The Fishy Dish kitchen.

"Somethin' smells fishy in here." Cal twitched his nose like Petunia when she got a whiff of ripe apples.

Meg spun around. "What are you talking about? You should be smelling something sweet not fishy." A few stray tendrils of hair framed her angry eyes. "I haven't started the chowder yet."

"That's exactly what I meant. *Fishy,* as in no fish smell in this Fishy Dish kitchen." Cal raised his eyebrows and waited for Meg to laugh. She didn't. "Sorry, it was supposed to be a joke."

Hannah shook her head. "Ignore him, Meg. I think his brain is scrambled from too much time at sea. All he has this morning are some lame jokes." Hannah inhaled near Meg's tray of yummies. "Whatever you just removed from the oven is making my mouth water with anticipation. Something knew?"

"I'm working on perfecting my grandmother's lemon square recipe and I think I've nailed it. Go ahead and let me know what you think." Meg lifted the parchment paper with the lemon squares onto a plate and sliced the big square into sixteen pieces.

"I'm going to let that cool for a few minutes. I want to enjoy your baking without a burnt tongue." Hannah helped herself to coffee and offered a cup to Cal. "Any activity from the guests yet this morning?"

"I saw that new guy, the photographer, walking on the beach back and forth with his phone to his ear. It must have been important from the way he waved his free hand around." Meg put a lemon square on two different plates.

Cal picked his up and nibbled a corner. "Ouch! Still hot."

"Has Gwen ventured out of the cottage yet?" Hannah asked, ignoring Cal's impatience.

A scream outside made all three jerk their heads toward the deck overlooking the ocean.

"What the heck?" Meg asked as she wiped her hands on her apron.

Cal was already halfway to the front of The Fishy Dish by the time Hannah heard his deep laugh. She looked around him to see a sight that was new but familiar.

Gwen stood frozen in place as Petunia grunted and snorted at her sandaled feet. The potbelly pig had an attraction to feet. Gwen's unnaturally tanned face had turned a shade of dirty ocean foam and her open mouth let out another shriek. "Is this pig going to eat my toes?"

"Only if they are smothered with nail polish," Hannah said with the straightest face she could manage.

Gwen's face changed from dirty foam to white seagull in color. Fortunately for her, Petunia lost interest in Gwen's toes and trotted through the snack bar toward the kitchen door.

"Oh no you don't," Meg said as she barricaded the kitchen door with her body. "You need to go to the *back* door like the dogs do."

Hannah helped Gwen move to one of the bar stools before her shaky legs dropped her tiny butt in the sand. "Harold told me I could find coffee down here. Do pigs roam free around this place?"

"Only this pig. You saw her yesterday at the photoshoot. That's Petunia and she's harmless."

"Unless she takes a liking to my nail polish?" Gwen's eyes were still as round as the sun climbing in the sky but her face had regained a bit of color.

"I was only teasing. Stay right where you are and I'll get you some coffee." Hannah disappeared into the kitchen where Cal and Meg were bent over double trying to control their laughing.

"How did Petunia know to make such a grand entrance at that moment?" Meg snorted through her laughter.

"Did you see her face?" Cal whispered. "I was afraid she was about to wet herself."

"Are you talking about Gwen or Petunia?" Meg asked.

Cal and Meg doubled over again, clutching their sides and laughing.

"Poor Petunia," Hannah said. "That shrieking would frighten any creature. See if you can find her a treat before I have to round her up and get her back to Ruby's house."

Hannah fixed a tray with coffee, cream, sugar, and a lemon square. "Any bets if this pencil-thin woman will eat the lemon square?"

"She will," Meg said. "Most don't stay thin by not eating, if you get my drift. Besides, if she doesn't eat it, I'll send Petunia back out there."

"I'll be sure to mention that for extra motivation." Hannah used her hip to push through the door.

Gwen still sat at the counter, her feet balanced his high as possible on the stool's rung. "There you are. I was going to try to make a mad dash back to the cottage and call for someone to deliver coffee to me."

"We aren't in the city so that's not an option."

Gwen hugged her arms around herself. "I can't believe Harold thought this was a good idea."

Hannah set the tray in front of Gwen and made herself comfortable on the stool next to her. "What's not a good idea?"

"This whole swimsuit photoshoot here in this rinky-dink town. He could have set it up anywhere, but no, he had to come here."

Hannah tried to hide her anger at the insult to Hooks Harbor being a rinky-dink town. That was one of the main attractions as far as she was concerned. And, she didn't correct Gwen about Harold setting up the photoshoot since Juliette had done that. Why Hooks Harbor, Hannah wondered.

Gwen poured about two drops of cream in her coffee, picked up the sugar but sighed and put it back down. "What's that?" She pointed to the lemon square.

"A complimentary lemon square. Try it. My baker said that if you don't, she'll send Petunia back out."

Gwen quickly picked up the lemon square and popped the whole thing in her mouth. Her eyes widened, closed, and a long sigh escaped through her lips. "Oh. My. Goodness. This is the best thing I've tasted for weeks." She licked off the tips of her fingers. "Don't tell Harold I gave in to a moment of weakness. He doesn't allow his models to eat anything much while we're working."

Hannah touched Gwen's arm in a gesture of friendship. "You're kidding. He tells you what to eat?"

"Not so much with words, but he gets the message across loud and clear with his expressions."

Hannah recalled Monique's order of a fish sandwich with no mayo or bread and her nervous laugh. "Do you like working for him?"

Gwen's hand flapped back and forth. "Well." She lowered her voice to barely above a whisper and peeked over her shoulder as if she suspected someone was eavesdropping. "Now that Monique is, um, out of the picture, I'm hoping Harold will help me move my career to the next level." She tapped her long red nails on the counter. "Or, I wouldn't mind being his girlfriend. There's lots of perks with that."

Like ending up at the bottom of a pool, Hannah thought as the image of Monique's body flashed through her brain. "So, Gwen, what do you think happened to Monique?"

"Seriously? That gold digging wife of his probably pushed her in, wiped her hands, and put on a worried face. We *all* saw how she attacked Monique after the dog incident. There was hatred in her eyes. And," Gwen checked behind her again, "Monique is the reason that marriage went down the drain. *I'd* want revenge if *I* was Juliette. Heck, she did me a favor. Harold's fair game now."

"You do realize how bad that sounds, don't you?" Hannah asked.

"I never pretended to like Monique. Why should I care if Juliette pushed her in the pool?" Gwen sipped her coffee.

"And you told all that to the police yesterday?"

"Of course. Why?"

Was she just plain dumb or brilliant? "The comments give you a motive. Do you have an alibi?"

Gwen blinked several times. "I didn't kill Monique. I was on break having a cigarette."

"Were you with anyone?"

She tilted her head in thought. "No, I guess I wasn't. Harold said I could take a break while he finished setting up. So I stood outside for a few minutes."

"The door close to the pool?"

"Yeah." Her eyes popped. "You think the police think that I followed Monique and pushed her in the pool?"

"It sure sounds like a possibility at the moment," Hannah informed her.

Gwen slid off the stool. "That guy at the Inn might have seen me when I was on my break. He more or less stalked me while I was there." She mumbled to herself as she walked away. "Calvin?

Coolidge? What was his name? Colin! I'll find him and tell him to give me an alibi."

Hannah shook her head as she watched Gwen converse with herself. Was she for real? Deputy Pam Larson must have had a field day while she questioned her.

Gwen left the snack bar and checked around the outside area before scooting as quickly as possible toward her cottage.

Hannah sensed someone behind her. "That was interesting."

"How so?" Cal asked. He held an extra-large piece of Meg's lemon square and offered a bite to Hannah.

"Gwen basically bragged about how great it is that Monique is, 'out of the picture,' her words. And I think she's going to work on an employee at the Paradise Inn to give her an alibi." She bit off a corner of the pastry. "Oh my. This is so delicious." She tried for a second bite but Cal pulled it out of her reach at the last moment before he laughed and let her have more.

"Does Gwen have any sense at all?" Cal asked. "Drumming up an alibi out of thin air is bound to backfire." He finished what was left of the lemon square.

"I don't know. She either has no sense or she's playing the dumb card for all it's worth." Hannah picked up the plate and cup that Gwen left on the counter.

"I'm going to rake the sand around the tables. Meg said to stop back in the kitchen before you get sidetracked with anything else. I'll be around for an hour or so if you have anything else you need help with." Cal wiggled his eyebrows. "Maybe we could rendezvous in your cottage?"

"Keep dreaming, Romeo." Hannah laughed and pushed her way through the kitchen door. Cal was one of the first people she met after she moved to Hooks Harbor and their friendship had blossomed into something special. Really special.

Meg had her pastries cut and arranged on a platter for guests and customers when Hannah walked back into the kitchen. Her clam chowder simmered on the stove and she was busy chopping a mountain of potatoes for her hand cut fries that were in huge demand.

"You haven't done anything about Jack yet. Caroline expects you to find out what's going on with him. Why he's avoiding her."

"I've been thinking about it. Now that I'm paying more attention, he does seem to be more tired than normal. Do you think there's some medical thing going on?"

"Heck if I know. I've known Jack for a long time but he never admits to any weakness to me. Maybe Pam would know." Meg pushed her cut potatoes into ice water to keep them fresh.

"I don't even dare ask her because if she doesn't know, she'll barge in and confront Jack and guess who will be on the short end of that stick?"

"Right. You. I guess you'll have to use your sleuthing tricks to figure it out."

"Or maybe my magic eight ball. At any rate, I'd better get Petunia back to her pen before she terrorizes someone else."

Meg snorted. "Served that city girl right. I haven't laughed that hard for too long." She waved Hannah out of her kitchen.

CHAPTER 14

Petunia had her own ideas about her day's activity and Hannah quickly discovered that it didn't include returning to her pen behind Ruby's house.

Armed with apple slices and plain popcorn, Hannah tried to tempt, bribe, and she even stamped her foot in frustration to get the potbelly pig to follow her up the road. Instead, Petunia trotted around each cottage, staying out of Hannah's reach as she rooted in the sand searching for her own treats.

Hannah gave up and went into her office to find Samantha. "Petunia has decided to stay here for a visit. Can you keep an eye on her?"

"Oh, that sounds perfect." Samantha fluffed up her curls. "Harold wants to do some more photos with me and Petunia. I'll let him know we're available."

"Good luck getting her to cooperate in the wide open. I don't know how she got out of her pen and she hasn't had complete freedom for a long time. She's loving it." Hannah dropped the harness, leash, and bag of popcorn on the desk. "She loves popcorn so maybe once she is finished investigating on her own, she'll get lonely and be more cooperative."

"Sit down for a minute." Samantha walked to the door and closed it. "I had an interesting chat with Vanessa this morning."

Hannah sat.

Samantha rested against the desk that had once belonged to Hannah's Great Aunt Caroline. An old oak monstrosity that dwarfed the petite woman. "First of all, she's furious that she is on the suspect list."

"Huh. I didn't even consider her but I suppose everyone with access to the wing at the Paradise Inn reserved by Harold would end up on Pam's suspect list."

"Right. She says she was in the shower. She always goes to shoots with Monique but since Harold was about to start his session, she decided she could take a break for a shower."

"That fits with what Ruby and I saw when we knocked on her door when we were looking for Monique. Vanessa was in her bathrobe with a towel wrapped around her head." Hannah puffed out her bottom lip. "But why did Vanessa always accompany Monique? It seems strange to me."

Samantha shrugged. "I guess they were close. Vanessa said they did everything together. She's devastated. Another thing she told me was that Gwen hated Monique. The two models were constantly trying to undermine each other for the best photos and, get this, for Harold's attention romantically."

"That's not exactly news after my conversation with Gwen this morning. Her words were, 'now that Monique is out of the picture,' she's hoping for more exposure and she wouldn't mind becoming Harold's girlfriend. She said there are a lot of perks that go with that role."

Samantha laughed. "Does she think ending up at the bottom of the pool is an attractive perk?"

"I guess she knows how to swim." Hannah cringed at her grisly joke. "Gwen is convinced that Juliette pushed Monique in the pool for revenge for breaking up the marriage. She basically said she would want revenge if it happened to her."

"So, there's no shortage of finger-pointing. Vanessa is pointing to Gwen, Gwen is pointing at Juliette, and what about Harold?"

"He's pointing to Juliette, and she thinks Harold is the murderer. Pam has her work cut out." Hannah stood. "Good luck with Petunia. I'll be back as soon as possible. With this mix of guests, I'm under no illusion that fireworks won't erupt round here at some point."

Before Hannah had a chance to make her exit, the door pushed inward and Deputy Pam Larson walked in. "Meg told me you might be in here."

"Hello Pam," Hannah said.

"It has come to my attention that you have some last-minute guests staying here that I need to ask more questions to."

"You must be referring to Harold Chandler III, Gwen Laine, and Vanessa Parkes?"

"Actually, I'm looking for Juliette Chandler. She disappeared yesterday before I had a chance to question her." Pam tilted her head and studied Hannah's face. "Are you hiding her here?"

"No. She's a grown woman and I have no control of her whereabouts. And for your information, she isn't renting one of my cottages." Hannah clenched her jaw.

This was so typical of how Pam needled her. They'd gotten off on the wrong foot after Hannah moved to Hooks Harbor and she didn't think they could ever become friends even though Jack was important to both of them. Jack assumed his daughter was jealous of his friendship with Hannah, but that wasn't something Hannah had any interest in changing.

"I'll rephrase my question. Do you know where I might find Juliette Chandler?" Pam gripped her cardboard coffee cup. Hannah thought there was a strong possibility that she might crush the cup if Hannah didn't give a good answer.

"As far as I know, she's at Ruby's house."

Pam smiled, a forced smile but better than the original glare. "That wasn't so hard." She turned to leave but stopped before she went through the door. "You spend time with my father." A statement from Pam, not a question. "Have you noticed anything different about him lately?" Her voice had softened and even hinted at a bit of vulnerability.

Hannah hesitated. Pam was part of the cover-up when Great Aunt Caroline was supposed to have died but Samantha didn't know anything about it. She couldn't share Great Aunt Caroline's similar concern about Jack. "No, but I'll keep your comment in mind the next time I see him."

Pam nodded and continued out the door and off the porch.

Hannah moved toward the door and saw Vanessa hurrying toward Pam with her hand waving in the air. "Oh, Miss Policeperson. Do you have a minute?"

Miss Policewoman? Pam's shoulders tensed. Hannah bit her lip to keep from laughing and took the opportunity to bypass Pam and Vanessa. Petunia also decided she was ready for a snack and ambled over to Hannah. She returned to her office with Petunia following behind.

"There's a change in plans," Hannah said to Samantha. "I'm taking Petunia to Ruby's house so I have an excuse for being there." She tilted her head toward Pam and Vanessa. "With some luck, she'll be tied up with Vanessa's problem and I'll have a chance to talk to Juliette again before Pam arrives."

Samantha put the harness on Petunia and clipped the leash to the ring. "I can get her when I know what the photo schedule timeframe is."

"Leave time to spray her down unless Harold wants a muddy pig on his calendar spread."

"I'll ask him." Samantha grinned. "I can imagine all kinds of scenarios with her—a bubble bath, a big tub of flowers, a pile of towels. This girl is on her way to stardom."

"Petunia or you, Samantha?"

"Both of us, of course." Samantha put one hand on her hip and struck a pose.

After a big handful of popcorn, Petunia was content to head down the road toward Ruby's house and her fenced-in pen. Nellie and Patches refused to be left behind. As they came abreast of Jack's house, Hannah glanced over and just made out his profile through the big front picture window. He looked to be asleep in his chair which was highly unusual. He wasn't normally a nap person.

Hannah picked up her pace as she detoured to Jack's front door. With a shaky hand she tried the doorknob without knocking, wondering if she should disturb him or let him nap. The door clicked and squeaked as she push it open.

"Can't I get any privacy without you barging in at all hours of the day?" Jack's cranky voice was music to Hannah's ears.

Hannah remained at the door with Petunia but the dogs let themselves in. "Just wondering if you want to come over to Ruby's house with us." She had to come up with some reason for dropping in.

"Us?"

"Yeah, me and Petunia. She's turned into an escape artist and I have to figure out how she got out of her pen. Want to help?"

Jack didn't answer. Hannah dropped the leash and rushed into the living room, his head tilted backward against the chair. His eyes were closed.

"Jack!" Hannah shook him.

His eyes opened but it took a few seconds for him to focus on Hannah's face. "When did you get here?"

"You don't remember?" Hannah crouched in front of Jack. "Are you feeling all right?"

He blinked a couple of times. "Yeah, yeah, don't hover. What do you want, anyway?"

Hannah straightened. "I guess you must have fallen asleep. I'm wondering if you want to come over to Ruby's house with me and help me repair Petunia's pen. Somehow she escaped this morning."

"Sure." Jack pushed himself up. "Do you think she'll have any coffee there?"

"Even if she does, you'll complain about it."

He headed into his kitchen. "I'll make some to bring. I can't stand weak coffee. It's meant to be strong and give a good caffeine kick." He busied himself measuring his coffee and water while Hannah waited.

"You don't have to wait for me. I can find my way down the road to your sister's house. You don't have to babysit." Jack turned his back to Hannah and turned his coffee maker on.

"Just keeping you company, Jack." Was he standing a little more stooped than normal? For his eighty-one years, he always stood ramrod straight, but something was a little different this morning. Her eyes roamed the kitchen—neat and tidy, except for some papers scattered on his small kitchen table.

She stepped closer. On top, rested an unopened envelope from a diagnostic laboratory. Her heart skipped a beat.

When Hannah looked back toward Jack, he was watching her with a scowl. "Don't be snooping into my business, Hannah."

"Jack, I'm not snooping. I care. What's in that envelope?"

"Well, how can I know? You can see plain as day that I haven't opened it yet." He returned his attention to his coffee and poured it into his big thermos.

"Is it bad news?" She held her breath.

Jack let out a loud, frustrated sigh. "Again, I haven't looked, so I can't answer any of your prying questions. Now, *drop* it and," he pointed his gnarly finger at Hannah, "don't mention or even hint at any of this to Pam. I don't want her over here twisting her hands and acting like I'm on my death bed or something. She hovers worse than you do. When I'm good and ready, I'll tell you what I want to share." He picked up the thermos. "Now, let's go and fix Petunia's pen."

Hannah snuck a last glance at the envelope but since she didn't have x-ray vision, she could only guess what was inside.

She left Jack's house with a knot in her stomach and fear in her heart.

CHAPTER 15

Petunia was nowhere in sight when Jack and Hannah left his house. Unlike her two faithful dogs who waited at the front door and danced around Hannah when she went outside.

"Nellie, why didn't you think to hang onto Petunia's leash?" Hannah jokingly asked her golden retriever mix.

Nellie looked at Hannah and wagged her tail even harder.

"Petunia's pretty smart. I bet she has already let herself back into her pen for a mid-morning nap," Jack said. "At least, that's what I'd be doing if I was her." He mumbled, "Peace and quiet away from all these hovering women."

Hannah smiled but pretended she didn't hear Jack's comment. As much as he complained, she suspected that he enjoyed the attention. Most of the time.

"I'll check the pen for Petunia if you want to take your coffee inside."

Hannah walked along the path that curved around the side of Ruby's house but not before she heard him mutter, "And bossy, too."

Wait until Great Aunt Caroline found out about Jack's unopened medical test. That was when he'd find out about bossy.

Hannah stopped at Petunia's gate. She was contentedly lying in the shade at the edge of her muddy puddle. She looked up at Hannah as if to say, *gee, what took you so long?*

Hannah jiggled the gate to find it firmly latched. Either she was smarter than Hannah realized, or someone found her and let her back into the pen. But how did she get out? Hannah took the leash and harness off the pig and turned toward her sister's house.

The back door of Ruby's house opened. "Juliette is gone!" Ruby shouted. "I took a shower while Olivia was watching Sesame Street and when I got done, she was gone."

Many possibilities ran through Hannah's brain. None of them good. And one she hadn't considered walked around the corner of Ruby's house just as Hannah reached the back door.

Pam's face was set like a stone statue—hard and cold. "Miss Chandler's car isn't here. I better not find out that you warned her that I was stopping by." Pam's eyes bore into Hannah's with a level of anger she hadn't seen before.

Jack walked out. "Cool down, Pam. Hannah was at my house until five minutes ago, and the only car that was here when we arrived was Ruby's. How about you come inside. I have some coffee."

Anyone who loved coffee and had ever tasted Jack's couldn't refuse his offer. And Pam probably went through ten cups a day, with nine of them being watered down dishwater from the police station.

She walked inside behind her father.

Maisy jumped on Hannah's legs begging for attention. Hannah bent down and picked up the small dog. "Where's your momma? She's coming back for you, right?" Maisy's tongue flicked out and caught Hannah's chin.

"Maybe I should lock up the dog to flush Juliette out of hiding." Pam's words were harsher than her tone but Hannah's arms tightened around Maisy.

With a deep sigh, Pam asked, "So, any idea where the elusive

Juliette Chandler might be?" Pam looked at Ruby over the rim of her mug.

"She's not Monique's killer," Ruby said.

"How about you help me find her and then let *me* figure that one out." The last part of her comment was pointedly directed at Hannah.

"I'm not sure where she is, but last night she said she had some unfinished business to take care of. She said that's why she scheduled this photoshoot in Hooks Harbor." Ruby looked at Hannah and raised her eyebrows. "She didn't give me any more details."

"Unfinished business like tracking down her husband to finish him off? Or that other model, Gwen?" Pam said.

"Nothing like that. She said it was connected to something that happened about six years ago. With another model." Ruby paused before she continued. "Juliette said she was doing a photoshoot at the cottages, now owned by Hannah, before she and Harold were married."

The hairs on Hannah's neck prickled. Great Aunt Caroline mentioned that incident and something about one of the models working for Harold leaving suddenly.

"I have a vague memory of that," Jack said. "Caroline commented to me at the time about how rude the photographer was to one of his models. She wanted to give him a piece of her mind but the one model left and the photographer was as sweet as sugar to the other one after that. Do you think it's the same guy who's here now?"

"I do," Hannah said forcefully before she caught herself and said too much about the information from Great Aunt Caroline who was supposed to be dead. "At least, according to what Juliette said to Ruby. I mean, how many photographers did Juliette work with?"

Jack gave Hannah an odd look but didn't grill her. The look told Hannah that he suspected she knew more than she was sharing.

"I'm going back to the station to do some digging," Pam said. "When—I'll be optimistic—when Juliette returns, tell her to get herself over to my office before I have to come here to drag her in." She lifted her cup toward Jack. "Thanks for the coffee, Dad. It's got me firing on all cylinders now."

Hannah put Maisy down after she was sure Pam was gone and wouldn't make good on her threat to take the dog. The Moodle immediately trotted upstairs and disappeared.

Jack made himself comfortable in Ruby's living room and kept his eyes on Hannah. She didn't like his intense scrutiny. She knew she'd have to confess to seeing Great Aunt Caroline as soon as they had privacy away from Ruby.

"Maybe I should have told Pam that Juliette left her bag here," Ruby said.

"She didn't ask so you're good," Jack said. "What she doesn't know can't hurt you."

"If anyone is going to snoop, I'd rather it be us. You know, just in case," Ruby said, leaving off what they all were probably thinking. Just in case there was something to incriminate Juliette.

"Lead the way. I'm happy to do the snooping honors," Hannah said. She seriously doubted that Juliette would leave anything incriminating at Ruby's house. But sometimes a distracted person forgets to be careful.

As Ruby led the way upstairs to her guest room, she whispered to Hannah, "Juliette did tell me something else that might mean something." She push the door open and let Hannah enter first.

Hannah made a quick visual inspection—the bed was made, a small carryon size case rested on a chair, and the start of a knitting project lay carefully rolled up on the bed with Maisy using it as a pillow. It didn't appear that Juliette left in a hurry or that she wasn't planning to return.

"Juliette told me that Harold admitted to her that Monique was driving him crazy. He regretted letting his, um, weakness, destroy their marriage." Ruby leaned against the doorframe.

"Do you believe it?"

Ruby shrugged. "Honestly, I don't know what to believe. I guess I don't know her all that well."

Hannah sat on the edge of the bed and picked up the knitting while she patted Maisy. "What's she making?"

"A blanket for Olivia. Dark pink, like Olivia requested." Ruby smiled. "She has a big heart, but—"

"But everything doesn't fit together nice and tidy, right?" Hannah finished Ruby's thought. "How did you meet Juliette?"

"A mutual friend. We hit it off right away and kept in touch. When she let me know she'd be coming to Hooks Harbor for a short stay, I was thrilled. She's the kind of person that even though we haven't known each other for more than a few years and hardly spend time together, it seems like we've known each other forever. It's weird."

"What about Harold? How well do you know him?"

"I met him a few times in passing. I had the impression that they were madly in love with each other. Frankly, I was shocked when she told me he wanted out of their marriage. I think it hit her like a ton of bricks and the one thing she's not willing to compromise on is Maisy."

Or possibly, letting another woman have what she still wants, Hannah added silently.

"Pam's going to have a field day when she finally sits down to question Juliette. Revenge is looking like a strong motive." Hannah carefully put the knitting back and stood. "Jack's probably wondering what the heck we're doing up here."

Ruby reached out to stop Hannah from leaving the guest room. "What about Harold? If Monique *was* driving him crazy, is it such a stretch to think he might have pushed her in the pool in a moment of, I don't know, extreme anger and frustration?"

"Not at all. That pool area was a revolving door for all the suspects. The question narrows down to why would Monique feel safe to go near the pool that she had such a phobia of?"

"Not with Juliette if they were enemies."

"Exactly what I'm thinking," Hannah agreed.

They wouldn't have walked in together, but Juliette could have followed Monique. If she was working through her fear, maybe she forced herself to walk past the pool. Anyone could have followed her. Including Juliette. Or Harold, or Gwen, for that matter.

Hannah hoped her thoughts were wrong.

CHAPTER 16

Jack made a quick examination of Petunia's pen before they left. The gate latch was secure and all the fencing was in place. Petunia watched them with the most innocent expression, if a potbelly pig could actually look innocent.

"She's smart, Hannah. You know what I think?"

"What?"

"She has figured out how to open the gate latch. Put up a monitor and see if you can catch her or whoever is helping her."

"That's a great idea. I'll ask Cal to do that for me."

They continued in silence toward Jack's house.

"Are you going to tell me what went through your mind when I asked Ruby if it was Harold staying at Caroline's cottages with Juliette six years ago?" Jack asked in the least pushy way possible.

"Who else would it be?" Should she tell Jack that she visited with Great Aunt Caroline? It would upset him to know they are talking about him behind his back.

"Don't answer a question with a question. That only confirms my suspicion. You've been talking to Caroline, haven't you?"

Hannah didn't look at Jack. She assumed her silence told him everything he wanted to know.

"I suppose I should have suspected that Caroline would contact you when I didn't answer her calls. Listen, I had some tests done and I'm not ready to see the results. I'm not even sure I *want* to see the results."

Hannah stopped walking and held Jack's arm. "It could be good news. You know, if the tests came back negative."

"I want to make up my mind how I'll proceed if it's *not* good news. Just in case." They started to walk again. "What else did you and Caroline talk about? Besides me?" He chuckled.

"We talked about the murder and when I mentioned the photographer's name was Harold, she remembered someone by that name stayed at her cottages six years ago."

"That's why you were so positive before."

"Caroline remembers that one of the models left. I'm wondering if this is somehow connected to the unfinished business Juliette referred to."

A car slowed and stopped next to Hannah and Jack. The passenger window rolled down. "I hope Ruby isn't mad that I left when she was in the shower. I couldn't handle a ton of questions." Juliette had a sheepish look on her face. "Am I safe to go back inside or is she planning to throw me and Maisy out?"

Hannah leaned down so she could look at Juliette through the open window. "What's going on Juliette? Where did you go? I understand you don't want a big inquisition but it might be a lot easier to talk to us before Deputy Larson finds you. She was over looking for you earlier and she means business."

Hannah didn't see any reason to pussyfoot around. Juliette was in deep trouble and if she thought she could evade the wave that was about to slam into her, she was in for an even bigger drenching than she realized.

Juliette's knuckles were white from her death grip on the steering wheel. "I had to talk to Harold. He called me this morning and I agreed to meet him on the beach."

That explains what Meg saw earlier—Harold on the beach

waving his arms while he talked on his phone. "And?" Hannah wasn't about to let that be the end of the conversation.

"He's willing to say he thinks Gwen killed Monique. He wants me to say I saw her go into the pool area."

"Did you?" Hannah's question came out as a fast exhale.

Juliette shook her head. "But if I don't say it, he'll tell the police that he saw *me* go into the pool area not long after Monique. The problem is, I don't know if he saw me or not."

"I saw you come out when Monique must have been at the bottom of the pool already. So, it's not a stretch that someone saw you go in. And I suppose it doesn't much matter. If you came out, you had to go in."

Juliette let her head rest on the steering wheel between her hands. "I don't know what to do."

Jack stuck his head next to Hannah's. "Listen to me. You tell my daughter the truth. Lying to her will get you nothing but more trouble. If you're innocent, don't act like you're hiding something. Get over to the police station and get it over with. That's my advice."

Jack smacked the roof of Juliette's car. "I'm going home."

"He's right, Juliette. Do you think Harold is asking you to lie because he killed Monique?"

"Or he thinks the police *think* he did."

"Consider this. If he asks you to lie for him, it might just be another way for him to make *you* look guilty." Hannah couldn't believe that she would even contemplate going along with Harold's plan.

"But he said he wants to get back together with me." Juliette looked at Hannah. Her eyes were filled with questions.

"He cheated on you once, Juliette. How could you ever trust him? And what about Gwen? She's ready to be his girlfriend as soon as he snaps his fingers."

A dark shadow flashed across Juliette's eyes.

Someone had to talk sense into this woman before she

completely messed up her life and decided to give Harold a second chance.

"Listen, Juliette. Stop at Ruby's house so she knows you're okay. Say hello to Maisy. She misses you. Then get yourself over to the police station and ask for Deputy Larson before she has to come looking for you."

Juliette nodded.

"And don't lie." Hannah moved back from Juliette's car and watched as she continued to Ruby's house. Harold was a snake and Juliette was acting like a scared mouse waiting to be his dinner.

Nellie and Patches decided the path to the beach appealed to them more than staying on the road. Hannah had no problem with their decision and followed behind the dogs.

Slipping off her flip-flops and burying her toes in the warm sand felt fantastic every time. Seagulls soared overhead and piping plovers skittered along at the edge of the waves. The briny scented breeze whipped her long braid over her shoulder as she picked up her pace to catch up with the dogs.

They charged ahead toward someone resting on a beach chair. As Hannah jogged closer, she heard a woman talking to Nellie. "Where did you come from you handsome girl?"

"Sorry. I hope they aren't bothering you," Hannah said as she stopped and was finally able to catch her breath.

The woman lifted her face toward Hannah. Vanessa's eyes peered through dark glasses. She quickly smacked her hand on her head to keep the wind from stealing her droopy woven hat. "They aren't a bother. I sure could use having my dog with me now but I have to leave her home when I'm traveling with Monique." She raised her free hand and quickly swiped across her cheek.

"Do you mind if I sit down for a minute?"

"No, of course not."

Hannah sat in the sand next to Vanessa's chair. "What do you think happened to Monique?"

Her shoulder's bobbed up and down. "Harold? Gwen? Juliette? Take your pick. They all had something to gain. At first I was sure it was Gwen, but, to tell you the truth, I'm not sure she's smart enough to plan something like that."

"Maybe it wasn't planned. Maybe everything fell into place in the moment."

"Huh, I hadn't even considered that possibility."

"Tell me, Vanessa. Why did you travel with Monique on these photoshoots?"

Vanessa took her sunglasses off and stared at Hannah. "Her phobia of course. Swimsuit shoots are always near water and I have to keep her calm and focused."

Hannah nodded. "So that's why you think this was all planned?"

"I guess so. Everyone knew about her fear of water, and recently Harold demanded Monique," Vanessa put her fingers up for air quotes, "get over it."

"And was she making any progress?"

"Baby steps, I guess you could say. That's the only explanation I have for why she would have been near the deep end of the pool. She must have been forcing herself to confront her fear." Vanessa sighed. "I guess, in a way, it's Harold's fault for pushing her to work on it to begin with."

"But it doesn't mean he *physically* pushed her in the pool." Hannah finished the idea.

"No, as much as I'd like to blame him, I think he genuinely cared for Monique."

That's interesting, Hannah said to herself. It didn't exactly agree with what Juliette told her, which made Hannah more and more suspicious of Harold and his motives for everything he was doing and saying.

Hannah stood and brushed the sand off the backside of her

pants. "I hope this spot helps you as much as it helps me when I have a problem."

"I'm thinking about Monique. You know, trying to figure out what I could have done differently."

Hannah nodded, not that Vanessa noticed since she was staring out to sea and stroking Nellie's silky fur.

"What about Juliette?" Hannah forced herself to ask. "Isn't Monique the reason Harold asked Juliette for a divorce?"

Vanessa shoved the sunglasses back over her eyes, effectively blocking Hannah from reading her emotions. "That's Juliette's version, but as far as Harold was concerned, that marriage was over well before Monique came into the picture."

CHAPTER 17

D elicious aromas drifted from The Fishy Dish, making
Hannah's stomach grumble. The lunch crowd drifted from
the beach into the snack bar to satisfy their seafood craving.
Samantha hustled between the picnic tables with trays loaded
with chowder, fried fish platters, and fish sandwiches.

Hannah grabbed a handful of Meg's hand-cut sweet potato
fries, lightly salted, and shoved them into her mouth.

"Here." Meg handed her a small bowl of chowder. "Take your
time. No one will starve to death before you get out there to help.
Samantha is actually keeping up quite nicely. I never know with
her lately, but today she's staying focused."

Hannah accepted the clam chowder gratefully. "I talked
to Jack."

Meg turned with her spatula hovering between a plate and the
grill. "And?"

"Don't say anything to him. He had some kind of medical
test done."

"He's waiting for the results?"

"Well…" Hannah hesitated. "He's got the results but he hasn't
opened them yet."

"I don't know anyone more stubborn than Jack. What's he waiting for?"

Hmmm. Hannah kept her thoughts to herself. Apparently, Meg didn't see herself as others did—stubborn *and* opinionated. "He's waiting until he has a plan on how to deal with the results if it's bad news."

"Get treatment! What's so hard about that?"

"I think he must be considering not going for treatment. Sometimes the side effects are worse than the diagnosis."

"This is a ridiculous conversation, Hannah. We don't even know what the test was for. Should I tell Caroline?"

"I'm not sure. She'll worry, and Jack doesn't want all of us hovering and wringing our hands and all that emotional stuff he's assuming we'll do."

"How about a good slap to knock some sense into him?" Meg's frustration oozed with her words. She finally remembered her fish on the grill and quickly flipped it onto the roll before it burned.

The door separating the kitchen from the front of The Fishy Dish swung open. "Gwen is leaving," Samantha said.

"Leaving town?" Hannah slurped down the rest of her chowder and put the bowl in the sink. "She can't leave if she's still a suspect." She pushed through the door.

Gwen perched on one of the counter stools with her phone to her ear. "Yeah. Pick me up at—" She looked at Hannah. "What's this place called?"

"The Fishy Dish."

"Pick me up at The Fishy Dish. As soon as possible. There are too many bugs and too much sand here."

Hannah wondered if Gwen preferred constant air conditioning, stale recirculated air, and artificial light to the beauty surrounding her which, apparently, she didn't notice.

She put her phone away and turned her attention to Hannah. "Don't tell Harold, but I've got a room back at the Paradise Inn.

Colin pulled some strings for me. He'll do anything for me." Her casual comment made Hannah suspect that with a flirty pout, Gwen was used to getting what she wanted from men.

Even murder? Hannah wondered as she looked at Gwen. She was showing her true colors—devious and manipulative. Did she use those special charms on Colin to get her rival *out of the way,* as Gwen referred to Monique's death?

"Isn't Harold planning some more shoots here at the beach?"

A noticeable quick tightening of Gwen's jaw muscles told Hannah that she was probably furious about whatever it was that Harold had planned.

"He said he doesn't need me today. He's got that pig scheduled to work with him." She glanced over her shoulder checking for any eavesdroppers in the vicinity. "And that old lady that tries to flirt with Harold. Between you and me? He's gonna be sorry that he's treating me with so little respect. A pig and an old lady instead of me?" She spat out the word *pig* as if her mouth was full of the sand she so hated getting lodged between her toes.

Gwen stretched out her long legs and slid off the stool. "My ride should be here." She dragged her large bag behind her toward the parking lot.

Hannah stared at the retreating figure. Wow. Just, wow, that anyone could feel so entitled. She almost hoped that Gwen was the murderer. She deserved to be punished for something.

A black Ford Mustang came to a screeching halt in a cloud of dust. Hannah wasn't too surprised to see Colin's profile in the driver's seat. She didn't know him well enough to know whether she should feel sorry for him or whether he and Gwen deserved each other.

He jumped out and managed to stuff Gwen's bag into the back seat of the Mustang. He ran around to the passenger side and opened the door for her while she inspected her nails. Hannah decided that Gwen was afraid she might break one of those long manicured nails if she attempted to open the door herself. They drove off and Hannah couldn't help but wonder what trouble would land in Colin's lap for being sucked into Gwen's web.

"Hey." Samantha elbowed Hannah in the side. "She's quite a piece of work, isn't she? Don't you ·kind of hope she's the murderer. Get those genes out of circulation?"

Hannah squinted at Samantha. "Interesting way to phrase it, but, yes, I was thinking along those lines, too."

"I'm pretty excited. Harold wants to photograph me and Petunia this afternoon." Samantha wiggled with pleasure. It reminded Hannah of Nellie's behavior when she was expecting something fun to happen.

"Gwen did share that scheduling tidbit. Her ego is badly bruised that you and Petunia are getting Harold's attention instead of her."

"What do you think I should wear? If these photos go into a calendar, I want to be sure I look my tip-top best!"

Hannah glanced down at her own casual t-shirt, shorts, and flip-flops. "You're asking *me* for fashion advice?"

"Good point. I'll talk to Ruby when I head over to give Petunia her bath. And if Juliette is around, she might be able to give me some pointers, too. I haven't felt this fidgety in years, Hannah."

Hannah turned away from Samantha and rolled her eyes. She hoped Samantha wasn't disappointed with Harold's plans. Or Petunia's cooperation level which could turn the whole affair into a disaster.

"I forgot to mention this before," Samantha said. "Pam called the office asking for you to swing by the police station." She raised her eyebrows for emphasis. "At your convenience."

"That sounds a bit too polite from Deputy Larson. I wonder what's up."

Samantha shrugged. "She didn't give me any extra details. Maybe she thinks your curiosity factor will get you moving quicker than if she left an ultimatum."

"Maybe."

Or, she wants to pick my brain about Jack. Boy, Hannah hated being in the middle of everyone's drama. First, she got sucked into Juliette's ugly divorce because Maisy melted her heart. And that mess went from ugly to deadly with Monique's murder. Now, she had to navigate between Jack and Pam. Nothing like being stuck in what felt like a no-win situation. And at the same time, she had to avoid a killer.

The only problem with that sensible line of reasoning was that she didn't know *who* the killer was.

Hannah parked at the police station and calmed herself with several deep breaths. Juliette passed behind her car, looking like she was in a hurry.

Hannah opened her door and called to her. "How did it go with Deputy Larson?"

Juliette's pale face turned toward Hannah. She blinked but didn't smile. Her cheeks puffed out before she sucked them back in. "Not very well, I'm afraid."

Hannah remained silent, hoping that Juliette would elaborate.

"The fact that I disappeared after Monique's body was found makes the deputy think I'm hiding something."

"She said that?"

"Not in those words, but all her questions were different variations of where did I go and why did I leave."

"Did you tell her about Harold and Monique's argument?"

"Yes, but that put me close to the pool so I think it may have done me more harm than good." Juliette's shoulders sagged. She ran her fingers through her hair. "I told her I saw Monique at the bottom of the pool because *you* told me not to lie, but as soon as I saw her eyes pop open with surprise, I knew I should have kept that to myself."

"I told you not to lie but you didn't have to offer information that she didn't ask for."

"She sort of did ask. She asked me if I knew where Monique was. The question caught me by surprise and since I hesitated, I knew she suspected something. So," Juliette flipped her hands up in defeat, "I didn't lie."

Hannah put her hand on Juliette's arm. "Don't worry, Pam will find the killer."

"I hope you're right because right about now, I think it's going to take some kind of miracle to get me out of this tangled web. If Harold pushed Monique in the pool, I'm sure he's devious enough to cover his tracks. If it was Gwen, I'm not sure about her smarts."

"I'm glad you didn't lie for Harold. That would have been a terrible strategy."

Juliette clutched Hannah's arm with a strong grip that dug her fingernails into her skin. "Please help me."

"I'll try, but I have some questions I want answered."

Juliette's hand fell to her side. "What questions?"

"From the last time you stayed in Hooks Harbor; when my cottages still belonged to my Great Aunt Caroline. Something happened then and I want to know if it's connected to what happened to Monique."

The last bit of color seeped from Juliette's face.

"I don't have time now, but I'll be expecting some answers," Hannah said without taking her eyes off Juliette.

"Soon."

CHAPTER 18

Pam had her back to her open office door when Hannah lightly rapped her knuckles on the wood. The deputy spun around. "Good, you got my message. Come in." She flicked her hand at the one empty chair opposite her desk.

Hannah sat and waited for Pam to get to the point of her request.

They stared at each other in a silent challenge.

Pam sighed. "My father. Did you find out anything?"

"Not really." Hannah decided that was the safest answer. It wasn't a lie and it didn't betray Jack. She looked away from Pam's steady stare. She didn't know what Jack's problem was and she knew he wouldn't want them talking behind his back. Especially if she told Pam anything that would be upsetting to her.

"*Not really*. That's about the wishy-washiest answer you could have given."

Hannah realized she gave herself away by averting her eyes. She looked at Pam again.

Pam's elbows rested on her desk with her fingers entwined. "You know something."

"I don't want to be in the middle of you and your father, Pam. Have you asked him if something is wrong?"

"No. He hates it when he thinks I'm mothering him. You know he doesn't like to show any weakness." She leaned forward, closer to Hannah. "Help me out. Should I be worried or am I just being paranoid about nothing?"

"I'm not sure. What I do know is that your father is," Hannah chose her words carefully, "waiting for information. He'll share it when he's ready." Hannah grinned. "My gut is telling me that we're all making a mountain out of a mole hill."

"Who all?"

"You, me…" Hannah mentally kicked herself. She didn't want to tell Pam that anyone else was worried about her father.

"And?"

"Great Aunt Caroline."

"She contacted you? Something must be wrong for her to get in touch with you."

"Caroline said that Jack wasn't returning her calls. She's suspicious. Like you. I don't want to start something that turns out to be nothing, but I saw an envelope on his table. It was from a medical lab."

"That sounds like something," Pam said. Her frustration was obvious.

"He hasn't opened the letter yet. He's not sure he wants to know what it says."

Pam slammed her hand on her desk. "That's ridiculous. If there's a medical issue, he needs to start treatment as soon as possible." Her reaction was eerily similar to Meg's.

"That's sort of what I told him, too. I think if it *is* bad news, he's not going to do anything. Or else, why wait? It's his decision in the end."

Pam quickly swiped the back of her hand across her cheek. "It's selfish. That's what it is." She looked at Hannah. "I can't imagine waking up one day without being able to stop at that curmudgeon's house first thing in the morning for the only decent cup of coffee I get each day."

"I suppose that's why he doesn't want you, or any of us, to know. He doesn't want all of us to hover and ask him how he's feeling and treat him differently."

"You're right, Hannah. Thank you for telling me. I won't say anything to my stubborn father." She smiled. "He's one of a kind."

"He is a special kind of special."

Pam smiled.

They both sat, lost in their thoughts for several minutes.

Hannah broke the silence. "Can I ask *you* something now?"

Pam's lip twitched and she rolled her eyes. "I suppose I owe you but I know *you* know I can't give you any information about the murder investigation."

"*Please.* I wouldn't even consider asking about *that.*" Actually, she was itching to ask about the conversation Pam just had with Juliette, but she chose to stay in a safe zone instead.

"As long as we have that clear, go ahead. What's on your mind?"

"Did you dig up anything about that other model that was staying at Caroline's cottage with Harold and Juliette six years ago?"

Pam leaned back, apparently relaxed now that Hannah was asking about a different case. "I researched Harold's photography business and there was an article published in the local paper about him. It was more of a personal interest story and it mentioned that Harold did a lot of shoots for swimsuit advertising and calendars, that sort of work, but there was no mention of the names of any models."

"We know Juliette was there. Did you ask her about it?"

"No. It never crossed my mind. I don't see any connection to what happen at the Paradise Inn to a model leaving suddenly six years ago."

Hannah pushed herself off the chair. "It would be a long shot." She turned to leave.

"Hannah?"

Hannah looked back at Pam. "You *will* let me know if you find out anything else about my father? Even if he tells you to keep your lips zipped?"

"If it's important, I'm sure he'll tell you himself when he's ready." Hannah hoped that answer satisfied Pam. She didn't want to agree to something she might not be able to do.

"You're clever with your words, Hannah Holiday. I'll give you that."

Without planning to, Hannah turned her car in the direction of the cottage where Great Aunt Caroline was staying. She didn't stop to think whether it was a good idea or not, she went on impulse.

As Hannah pulled in behind the tidy cottage, she hoped that more memories had returned to Great Aunt Caroline about Harold and Juliette's visit when they stayed at her cottage six years earlier. Hannah knew it was unlikely, but there had to be an important reason why Juliette was dredging up that visit. It was possible there was a connection. But what?

As Hannah followed the path around to the front of the cottage, Great Aunt Caroline sat on a swing in the shade of a hemlock tree. It was strategically located to be hidden from most eyes. She held a book in her lap, and her feet kicked the ground to keep the swing in motion. The rhythmic squeak of the swing matched the in and out of the waves. Caroline didn't look up as Hannah approached.

The setting was peaceful and she hated to interrupt Caroline's quiet moment but she stepped closer.

Great Aunt Caroline's hand moved to her forehead shielding her eyes from the sun. "Hannah? What are you doing here? Is it Jack?" The book slid off Caroline's lap and thudded on the ground.

"No. Jack is…working through a decision." Hannah sat on the swing next to her great aunt.

Caroline's touch on her arm felt like the soft flutter of butterfly wings.

Hannah sighed. "He has an unopened letter with medical test results."

Caroline nodded. "He doesn't want treatment if it's bad news. He and I have talked about this. I'd probably make the same decision. Is that what you came to tell me?"

"That and something else. I'm wondering if you remember anything else about when Harold, the photographer, stayed at your cottage with some models. Yesterday, you said he was rude and one of them left. Was there anything else?"

Caroline leaned her head back and closed her eyes. Her feet kept the swing moving back and forth. A lobster boat moved along the water in front of the cottage, stopping at buoys to pull up his lobster traps.

"Harold was on the beach with his camera berating the model that she had gained too much weight. I was horrified, Hannah. The woman was beautiful, with curves, and long brown hair. I can still see her face. It was frozen into a mask. Her emotion hidden. Then she pointed at Harold but I either never heard what she said or I've forgotten. All I could think was that I wanted to put my arm around her, comfort her, and tell that horrid man what I thought of him."

"That model wasn't Juliette?"

"No. That woman left and, afterwards, Harold was as charming as a prince toward Juliette. I still regret that I didn't find out more details." Caroline turned to look at Hannah. "You think that incident has something to do with what happened at the Paradise Inn?"

"I think I'm grasping at straws. All I know is that Juliette told Ruby she scheduled this photo event here in Hooks Harbor six months ago, before Harold told her he wanted a divorce. She said she had some unfinished business to clear up. Something that happened six years ago."

"Hmm." Caroline put a finger curved with age to her lip. "Could she be trying to track down that other model?"

Hannah stretched her arm along the back of the swing and straightened her legs out in front, keeping them off the ground. "That or track down someone who knew her. Maybe she was hoping to talk to you or look back at the guest list."

"The guest list! That's a good place to start. I always had a guest sign-in book in the office. It will take some digging, but if Juliette remembers the dates, you could narrow your search down."

"If that model signed the book."

"Yes. If."

"Where did you store those books?" Hannah was mentally going through all the boxes Great Aunt Caroline had left for her, and guest books weren't part of the memory.

"Jack should have them in his basement. I had limited space for storage and that kind of thing didn't seem important but I couldn't bring myself to dump them either. I'm sure Jack will still have them." Caroline stopped the swing and bent down to pick up her book. "You don't happen to have any books in your car, do you? They are great company for me these days."

Hannah stood and stretched. "Actually, I do have a box of books I've been planning to drop off at the library for their next book sale. I'll get them."

"Hannah? Before you go, give me a hand, please. These old joints tend to stiffen up and I have a bit of trouble getting out of this swing on my own."

Hannah frowned. "What would you have done if I didn't just happen to stop by?"

She laughed. "Waited until someone did show up."

Hannah pulled Caroline to her feet and it felt like she was as light as a feather. "That sounds like a terrible plan."

"Don't look so worried. Meg comes over every day to bring me dinner. I told her to bring food for several days but she wouldn't listen. I think she really only wants to check and make sure I haven't keeled over dead in her brother's cottage. Wouldn't that be a shock around town? I can imagine the headline: *Dead woman dies a second death in ocean-front cottage.*"

Caroline found great pleasure in that potential mystery but Hannah didn't laugh. Going through Caroline's death once was enough even though she knew she would have to face it again someday.

Hannah helped Caroline into the cottage before she retrieved the box of books. "I hope there's something in here that appeals to you. I'm a fan of mysteries, so this is a collection from cozies to thrillers."

"That doesn't surprise me since you take on these real-life mysteries all the time. Personally, I don't like anything too gory but a nice light entertaining whodunit will keep my mind busy without giving me nightmares."

Hannah hugged her great aunt, careful not to squeeze too tightly. She felt so fragile under her cotton sweater.

"Give my best to Jack and tell him if he doesn't pick up the phone the next time I call, I'll be knocking on his front door in the middle of the day for all the neighbors to see." Caroline cackled. "I miss that old curmudgeon. Tell him to come visit. Soon. Before one of us is dead."

CHAPTER 19

Jack was napping on his comfy recliner when Hannah let herself in. At least that was what it looked like he was doing. Without opening his eyes, she heard him say, "I'm trying to get some peace and quiet but you just barge in anyway. Don't you have any manners?"

"I have a message for you but with that attitude, I'll leave instead." Hannah headed back toward the front door.

His eyes popped open. "A message?" He sat up straight. "Get back in here, Hannah Holiday. Did you visit Caroline again?"

"Are you psychic?" She looked at him with her hands on her hips. "Yes, as a matter of fact I did, and she had a great suggestion about where to look for information about the time Harold stayed at the cottages six years ago."

He snapped his fingers. "Of course. The guest sign-in books," he said before Hannah had a chance to tell him. "I should have thought of that already. I've got them all in the basement, organized by date. Do you know the date we're looking for?"

"No. Great Aunt Caroline thought it was six years ago."

Jack stood. He massaged his lower back a couple of times. "Let's go take a look. With both of us going through the signatures, it shouldn't take too long. Of course, there's no guarantee that there even is a signature. Not everyone signed the book."

"Jack?"

He turned around and faced Hannah. His eyes read her expression. "You told her, didn't you? You told Caroline about the lab test."

Hannah ignored the actual question and delivered Caroline's message. "Her message is that if you don't pick up the phone the next time she calls, she's coming over here in the middle of the day. She wants you to visit." Hannah lowered her voice. "Before one of you dies."

"Ha! Caroline is already dead. She can't die again." He tried to make light of the subject but his chin trembled slightly.

"She had a comment about that, too. She's already written the headline for when the day comes: *Dead woman dies a second death in ocean-front cottage.*"

Jack shook his head. "That one has a sick sense of humor. What should we do about her?"

"Go visit, Jack. She does have a point. Spend as much time together as you can."

"Oh, don't go getting all maudlin on me, Hannah Holiday. If your Great Aunt Caroline didn't pull off that whole death thing, you wouldn't even be living here. Did you remember that?"

"Yes." Hannah's voice was barely a whisper. Now that she knew the truth about Caroline's living status, that fact was never far from her thoughts. She could be back in California with a failing dog walking business. But she refused to let Jack make her feel guilty about a plan that she had absolutely nothing to do with. "Let's look for that guest book." She headed for the cellar door without looking back to see if Jack was following.

She flipped the light switch up. She licked her lips and dried her clammy hands on her pants. A warm light flooded the basement. Good lighting at least, she thought. Basements had never been her favorite place to wander around. Too many cobwebs, damp floors, and just the whole underground part made her queasy.

Jack bumped into her. "Well, are you going down the stairs or do I have to push you?"

Hannah turned her head to glare at Jack. "Don't even try to make a joke."

Jack's jaw dropped. "You're scared? Your jaw muscles are working overtime. You don't want to go into the basement." It wasn't a question. He read her face.

Hannah's voice dropped. "My father locked me in the basement once. He thought he was teaching me a lesson, but—"

Jack pulled Hannah away from the cellar door. "Don't even tell me more. I don't want to know how he thought he could justify something like that. Call Ruby and tell her to come over and help me find the right year."

With shaky fingers, she pulled her phone from her back pocket. The call went straight to voicemail. "No answer. She either has her phone turned off or the battery is dead. I'll just run over to her house."

Hannah couldn't get out of Jack's house quickly enough. Looking down the basement stairs had made her chest tighten. As soon as she was outside, she sucked in the fresh air, calming the panic that had almost taken over. She let out one last long exhale, shook her hands, and walked to Ruby's house.

Hannah found Ruby and Samantha in the backyard. She burst out laughing at the sight of their antics. Ruby held the hose while Samantha used a soft brush to loosen the mud off Petunia's sides. Petunia held her snout in the air and Hannah was sure she heard a contented grunt and groan. Maisy danced around the whole affair, dashing in and out to lick water dripping off Petunia.

"You should invite Harold over here to get shots of this scene. It might not win a beauty award, but I think it might get first place for comedy."

Samantha glared and used her shoulder to push some stray hairs out of her face as she kept on scrubbing.

"I think Petunia rolls in the mud just so she gets this special spa treatment," Hannah teased.

"I want her to look her *best* for the photos; not like she belongs at some amusement event," Samantha said as she huffed and puffed and worked off the mud. She straightened. "How does she look?"

"Great, but you'd better have Ruby turn that hose on you, Samantha. You've got mud splattered from your cheeks to your toes."

Samantha rubbed her face and looked down. "Great. I was supposed to be back at the beach ten minutes ago. Can I hop in your shower, Ruby?"

Ruby angled the hose up so a nice spray fell over Samantha. "Sure."

"Hey!" Samantha jumped away from the water. "A hot shower in your house, you ninny. Not this ice water."

As soon as Samantha leaped to the side, Petunia spooked and took off down the road.

"This is all your fault, Hannah. Ruby and I were doing great until you showed up. What am I supposed to do now?" Samantha's bottom lip puffed out. She even sniffled.

"Go take your shower. I'll head Petunia off at The Fishy Dish. I'm sure she'll go there first looking for a treat from Meg." Or a customer eating something tasty, she said to herself. She turned to Ruby. "Can you go to Jack's house? He needs help finding something in the basement."

Ruby's eyebrows jumped up under her bangs. "Were you going to help him?"

Hannah nodded.

"Did you have a panic attack?"

"Yes. Can you help? I can't believe that old fear snuck up on me again after all these years."

Ruby turned off the faucet and coiled the hose. "What is he looking for?"

"Great Aunt Caroline's guest sign-in books."

"Okay. You must be hoping to find the name of that other model. I asked Juliette but she was evasive. Something weird happened during that visit."

The two sisters walked together until Ruby turned into Jack's driveway and Hannah continued alone to her snack bar. Even if they found the name of the model, how would Hannah track her down? Why was Juliette protecting her? Would she be able to tell them anything that might connect to Monique's murder? Those questions had no answers. Yet.

As she neared the outside picnic tables, she heard a screech. Great. Petunia must be after someone's feet again.

Hannah jogged through the parking lot. What met her eyes was even funnier than Samantha giving Petunia a bath. Both Gwen and Colin huddled together on top of one of the picnic tables while Petunia stood with her front feet on the bench seat and tried to reach Gwen's toes. Actually, Colin crouched behind Gwen and continued to eat his ice cream cone. Really? And Gwen expected Colin to help her with an alibi for Monique's murder?

Hannah picked up the end of Petunia's leash and pulled her back so she had to drop her front feet off the seat. "I hope you didn't give her your ice cream," she said to Gwen.

"I didn't have any." Gwen lowered her voice and looked around. "Well, I had a couple of licks of Colin's, but don't tell Harold."

Hannah used her thumb and index finger to zip her lips closed. "Of course not. Petunia seems to have taken quite a liking to you, Gwen. Maybe Harold will want you in the photos with her."

Gwen's carefully-plucked eyebrows lowered, causing a big wrinkle to form between them. "He can't pay me enough."

Colin, regaining his courage as soon as Hannah had Petunia

under control, jumped off the picnic table and extended his hand to help Gwen climb down. "So, it's all set? I was with you at your break when everyone was looking for Monique?"

"Oh, Colin. I'm glad you remembered. And you told that policewoman, right?" Gwen rubbed her hand up and down Colin's arm.

Hannah felt like throwing up as she watched Gwen manipulate the poor guy. Was he so desperate for a date that he'd lie for her to the police? "Gee, Colin, I remember seeing you talking to Ruby when everyone was looking for Monique. How could you be in two places at once?"

Gwen's eyes narrowed as she pulled her hand away from Colin. She took a step away not realizing she was moving closer to Petunia, but Petunia didn't miss the opportunity to stick her moist nose on Gwen's bare toes.

Gwen's mouth opened but nothing came out. For about six long seconds.

Then an ear piercing scream almost broke Hannah's ear drums.

But it was worth it to see Gwen jump back up on the picnic table in one leap.

And the look on her face when Deputy Pam Larson pulled into the parking lot was the icing on the cake.

Colin mumbled something about needing to get back to work.

"Are you still taking me to dinner tonight, Colin?" Gwen yelled as he headed toward his car.

He glanced quickly back at Gwen. "I'll pick you up at five." Then he diverted his eyes and hustled past Pam as *she* headed straight toward the snack bar.

It was impossible for Hannah to miss Colin's nervous behavior, but what puzzled her the most was the cause.

CHAPTER 20

P am greeted the teenager working for Hannah at the ice cream window of The Fishy Dish. Having summer help was priceless as far as Hannah was concerned, especially when she found such a motivated and hardworking teenager. "How's it going, Chelsea? Are there any new flavors I might like?"

"Hello, Pam," Hannah said before Chelsea had a chance to respond. "You might like Udder Chocolate Chip Delight. It's been my most popular flavor so far."

Pam licked her lips. "That sounds too good to pass up. I'd like a double on a waffle cone, please." She turned facing the ocean and leaned against the counter. "Anything new with my father?"

Hannah shook her head. "Nothing he has felt the need to share with me. Anything new with your investigation?" She didn't expect any information but it couldn't hurt to ask.

Pam smiled. "I just stopped at Dad's house. He and your sister were looking through some interesting books...of Caroline's."

"Here you go, Deputy Larson." Chelsea handed a mountain of ice cream to Pam and accepted her money. "I'll get your change."

"No need. Add it to your college fund, Chelsea." Pam moved

away from the ice cream window, licking her cone before it had time to drip all over her hand.

Hannah followed.

"This is delicious. Good recommendation." Pam stared at the ocean.

"About the investigation?" Hannah prompted.

"Oh yeah, that's what we were talking about. How about we help each other out? You tell me if you discover the name of the model who was staying here with Juliette and Harold six years ago. Searching in Caroline's old guest books was a brilliant idea, by the way. I'll tell *you* that alibis are starting to pour in." Pam licked her cone but kept her eyes squarely on Hannah's face.

"What alibis?"

"What's the name?"

"I don't know, but I'm happy to share it with you if we figure it out."

Pam enjoyed a bite of the waffle cone. "Do you really think it will help pull Juliette out of the deep hole she's gotten herself into?"

"I don't know the answer to that either, but I do think it will help shed light on the current mystery. Only time will tell who it helps or hurts."

Pam nodded. "I'm glad you have an open mind because I'll share this with you, Hannah, Ruby's friend has a lot of explaining to do."

Hannah forced her voice to stay calm. Pam always knew just how to push her buttons. "What about Harold? He said Monique was driving him crazy. And what about Gwen? Now she doesn't have any competition for the modeling jobs with Harold or for becoming his newest girlfriend. Or, even Colin who, I think, might be lying for Gwen."

Pam's eyebrows shot up and she choked as she finished swallowing the last of the waffle cone. She pounded her chest. "That's news," she blurted out as soon as she could talk again. "What do you mean, he might be lying?"

"Okay...I don't know what the truth is, but Gwen told me she was going to ask Colin to say he was with her when she was on her break."

"Uh-huh."

"I was with Ruby when Colin was discussing Monique's disappearance with her. He was in the hall outside the main door for the pool area, not where Gwen said she was taking her break which was near the opposite door."

Pam wiped her fingers on her khaki pants and pulled a notebook and pen out of her breast pocket. She jotted some notes. "I'm still waiting to get the security videos. That might clear up some of these conflicting stories of who was where when. In the meantime, don't forget to get me that model's name when you uncover it."

Pam walked to the picnic table where Gwen sat touching up the red on her fingernails. At the same time, Harold made a big detour around the picnic table toward Hannah.

"You have the pig, but where's Samantha?" He checked the time on his phone. "I told her to meet me here a half hour ago. What happened? Are you filling in instead?"

"First, Mr. Chandler, this is Petunia, not *the pig* as you refer to her. Got it?"

Harold opened his mouth but Hannah continued without giving him a chance to reply. "If you plan to photograph her, she needs a contract like any other model you hire."

He snorted. "You're kidding. The only four-legged model that has a contract with me is Maisy, and I expect that will change once Juliette gets arrested for killing Monique."

"What makes you so sure of yourself about that?"

"Oh, come on. Just because she gave you some sob story about how I mistreated a model before she and I got married doesn't mean I killed Monique. Juliette is the one with a strong motive to kill her. After all, Monique is the reason our marriage fell apart. And, besides, Juliette walked right through the pool area."

Hannah's ears pricked up at the mention of Harold's past treatment of a model. "Your past might come back to haunt you when that model reveals herself and the sordid details of that harassment charge." Hannah had no idea what she was talking about but if she pretended she had knowledge of some details, maybe she could force Harold's hand.

He leaned close to Hannah's face. She smelled a combination of fish breath and suntan lotion. It was nearly as unpleasant as the sneer on his face and almost made her gag. "If she dares to come out of whatever rock she's been hiding under, she'll be subjecting herself to a lawsuit that she won't win. I made sure of that."

"Yoo-hoo! Harold, sorry I'm a tad late. Oh good." Samantha stopped next to Hannah and took a few seconds to catch her breath. "You have Petunia." She took the leash. "Where do you want to do the photographs?"

Samantha blinked her eyelashes that looked longer than usual, in Harold's direction. Her red flowery skirt was tied at her waist with a short sleeve top of matching fabric flowing just even with the waistband. Her hand held a straw hat, and big sunglasses shielded her eyes. She smiled.

Harold turned away from Hannah as if he was dismissing an unruly child. "Let's have the two of you sit at the picnic table. Sharing an ice cream. I want this to be about food, fun, and frolicking."

"Ooooh," Samantha squealed. "This is going to be so much fun." She linked her arm through Harold's and let him lead her as she led Petunia to a picnic table.

"How about under a red umbrella instead? I think it matches my outfit better than this blue one." Samantha moved to a different table.

Harold approached the ice cream window and ordered a bowl of vanilla. By the time he returned, Samantha was settled on the picnic table bench. As soon as the ice cream appeared, Petunia eagerly jumped up with her front feet and tried to stick her nose in the bowl.

"Hold on Petunia. I'll give you a little taste. Too much will be bad for your figure."

Harold scooted around to the other side of the table with his camera. "Feed her with the spoon."

Samantha dug the spoon into the creamy deliciousness and held it for Petunia to lick.

"Good." He moved into different positions and angles with his camera clicking as Samantha shared the ice cream with Petunia. When a breeze threatened to blow her hat away, she held it on Petunia's head. The sunglasses were next to complete Petunia's casual beach look.

"Perfect. You two are naturals." He continued to click away.

It was good that Ruby arrived with Jack, Olivia, and the three dogs before Hannah ruined Samantha's fun with talk of a contract. That problem could wait for a bit she decided when she saw that Jack was carrying a book.

"We found it." He dropped the book on the counter in The Fishy Dish. "I'll be right back."

Nellie and Patches made themselves comfortable in some shade.

Jack went to the ice cream window with Olivia. "What flavor do you want today?"

Ruby sat next to Hannah. "He spoils her rotten but I don't want to say anything because...well, look at them."

Hannah watched as Jack lifted Olivia up so she could see all the ice cream flavors. She pointed to one. Jack nodded and gave the order to Chelsea. He crouched down to Olivia's level and let her sit on his knee. Maisy made herself comfortable leaning against Olivia's legs.

"See what I mean?" Ruby said. "Those two are a sight for sore eyes. I'm never sure which one is taking care of the other—six year old Olivia, or eighty-one year old Jack."

The two sisters stared for several minutes until Ruby turned her attention to the book in front of Hannah. "We think we found the name."

Hannah flipped the book open where she saw a piece of paper marking a page. Her finger slid down the left page and she scanned the names, then her finger moved to the signatures on the right page. She stopped about halfway down on Harold Chandler III, of course he added the III, and his comment was pure advertising: *the best photography forever.* Below was a signature for Juliette Hale and the comment: *the perfect place to fall in love.* "Was Hale her maiden name?"

Ruby nodded.

Hannah's finger moved down one more line. "Candace V. Jones? *This beauty helps to offset everything that has gone wrong.*" She looked at Ruby. "How do we know this isn't just any old guest?"

Ruby shrugged. "That's why I said *maybe* we found the name." She pulled the book in front of her and pointed to the names Hannah had just mentioned. "All three signed the book on the same date with black ink. Before and after, the signatures are in blue ink."

"Okay. That does sort of lump them together, but now what?"

"That is the million-dollar question isn't it?" Ruby slid the book back to Hannah.

"I'm going to show this to Pam. She can use her resources to track down this person, and while she's doing that, we're going to ask Juliette who Candace is."

"I've tried to get her to open up about her stay here six years ago but she always changes the subject," Ruby said, her tone filled with frustration.

"Right, but now we have a name and if it's the right name, she won't be able to hide her emotions."

Hannah glanced at Olivia and Jack sitting outside with their ice cream. Theodore was propped up on the table as Olivia ate and chattered away. Maisy sat on the bench next to Olivia and after every few bites that went into Olivia's mouth, Maisy got a taste too. "I hope you aren't too concerned about dog germs."

"It's a little too late now, don't you think?" Ruby chuckled.

"Harold said something interesting to me just before you got here. He seemed to think Juliette did share her sob story with us about how the model allegedly accused Harold of mistreatment. I pretended to know what he was talking about and asked him what he'd do if she came out about the harassment."

"And?"

"He said he'd sue her. My guess is that he paid her off to keep her quiet. Maybe he paid Juliette off, too. She's hiding something and it's about time she shares what she knows. Pam hinted that Juliette needs a miracle to dig herself out of the hole she's in, and this name might not be a miracle but it could be a sliver of hope for her."

Juliette was outside with her laptop when Ruby and Hannah returned to Ruby's house. She slammed it closed as soon as she realized they were next to her.

"So, Juliette," Hannah began, "who is Candace?" Hannah decided shock might be the only strategy that could get through to Juliette about the serious problem she faced.

Juliette's eyes popped open wide before she diverted her gaze away from Hannah. "I don't know who you're talking about." She swung her legs off one side of the lounge chair and stood, tense and ready to flee.

Hannah held her arm. "I think you do and it's time you level with us unless you have some nice striped jail clothes picked out."

Ruby took Juliette's other arm. "Let's go inside and talk. Hannah already gave the name to the police and they'll track her down one way or another."

Hannah felt Juliette's arm relax. Her shoulders and head

sagged. "I've been wanting to get this off my chest but I didn't want to burden you with my problem, Ruby."

"It's still your problem, but knowing more about what happened between Candace and Harold might help you," Hannah said.

CHAPTER 21

Ruby made iced tea for the three of them while Juliette began her story. "It was my first modeling job with Harold and I wanted so desperately to make a good impression. You know, I was young and full of dreams and I thought I deserved to be a top model."

Ruby set a tray with the drinks on the coffee table in front of Juliette.

"Candace was older, more experienced, and I resented her even being around Harold." She sipped her drink. "I wanted all his attention for myself and I saw Candace as competition."

"Had Candace worked with Harold before?" Hannah asked.

"Yes. I started to notice something weird going on between them. And then Candace always insisted on being near me so I was never alone with Harold." Juliette twisted her hands anxiously. "She got on my nerves, to say the least. The tension got so thick, I thought I would choke on it. The two of them had a terrible fight and the next day, just like that," she snapped her fingers, "Candace was gone."

"She never said anything to you about what was going on with Harold?" Hannah asked.

LYNDSEY COLE

Juliette shook her head. "I wouldn't have listened anyway because I was completely blinded by Harold at the time. If only I'd had the sense to ask her more about him I could have saved myself years of pain. As soon as Candace was gone, Harold became attentive to me, took tons of photos, promised to make me famous." She looked at Hannah then at Ruby. "He said everything I wanted to hear and I never questioned any of it. I couldn't believe my good fortune when he asked me to marry him."

"Until?" Hannah prodded.

"You're right. Until the next young model caught his eye. And then I started to realize I wasn't so special and maybe what happened to me when Monique showed up was exactly what happened to Candace when I showed up." She sighed as if she was relieved to finally get that story off her shoulders.

"Harold said something to me today that made me think that maybe he paid Candace to leave. Paid her to be quiet. Do you think she had some information on him?" Hannah asked.

"I don't know. I was hoping I could track her down and ask her what exactly happened but I haven't had any luck. It's like she disappeared into thin air. How did you figure out her name?" Juliette tilted her head. "Did Harold tell you?"

"Ha! I'm pretty sure he doesn't want any of us talking to her. You all signed the guest book when you stayed at the cottages six years ago. We dug it out of my friend's basement and went through, page by page, until we spotted Harold's and your signatures. We made a lucky guess that the next name was the other model staying with you two. It was a bit of a bluff when we asked you about Candace."

"And I bit," Juliette said. "Is it true that you gave the name to the police?"

"Not yet, but now that you've confirmed her identity, I will pass the information on."

Juliette massaged her neck. "I don't know how this can help. It

136

was six years ago. What would that have to do with what happened to Monique?"

Hannah drained her iced tea and stood. "I'm not sure, but at the least I would say that Mr. Harold Chandler III has a history of using women and throwing them out with the dishwater when he gets bored. You said Candace didn't want you to be alone with Harold?"

"Yeah. I thought she was jealous and was protecting her territory."

"Maybe she was protecting you, Juliette. Maybe Harold has a darker side than just moving from one woman to another."

"Like murder?" Juliette whispered.

"Maybe not murder, but there are many forms of abuse that women keep hidden."

Juliette nodded. "He does have a quick temper and said horrible things sometimes but then he would always apologize and he would be sweet and kind. As time went on, I thought I was living with two different people. But it happens slowly and you get used to it."

Ruby moved next to Juliette. "Monique may have done you the biggest favor in the world by catching Harold's eye. You're almost done with him with no strings attached, remember?"

"Except for Maisy. If he knows I've talked to either of you about this, he said I'd never see my Maisy again." Juliette looked around the room in a sudden panic. "Where is she?"

"With Jack and Olivia. They'll take good care of her. Don't worry."

Juliette jumped off the couch. "I need to get her. I'm supposed to be with her to keep her safe. If Harold sees her and I'm not around, he might take her just to punish me."

The hairs stood on Hannah's neck. Harold was at the beach photographing Petunia and Samantha while Olivia had ice cream. It was an idyllic scene but a scene with an underlying potential for trouble. Maisy could easily wander over to Harold and there was no knowing what he would do.

"I'll walk back to The Fishy Dish with you." Hannah kept her voice calm even though her stomach had already twisted into a knot of concern for Maisy. The picture of Harold that was beginning to emerge gave her more than chills.

"I'll go too. I don't want Jack to be stuck with Olivia for too long." Ruby quickly glanced at Hannah with her eyebrows raised and her mouth turned down. Hannah understood that Ruby also suspected the potential danger Maisy was in.

Nellie and Patches, happy to be outside again, raced ahead to the snack bar as soon as they saw which way Hannah turned out of Ruby's driveway. Hannah heard Nellie's alarm bark and she picked up her own pace. "Something's wrong. I hear it in Nellie's bark."

As they neared the parking lot, Vanessa was pulling on Harold's car door and screaming. "Let her out. She's frantic."

It didn't take long to figure out who Vanessa was talking about. Nellie had her front paws on the back door as she continued to bark. Patches howled. With all that noise, at first, Hannah didn't hear Maisy's high pitched yipping.

The three women surrounded Harold's car, forcing him to make a decision to turn it off or run one of them over. Hannah didn't budge as she stared through the windshield of Harold's car. Her body tensed and she hoped she could leap out of the way if he hit the accelerator. She counted the seconds with each beat of her pounding heart.

Harold shut his car off.

Juliette tried to open the back door to rescue Maisy, but it was locked. She opened the driver side door and reached for the master unlock button before Harold had a chance to stop her. When the locks clicked, Vanessa pulled the back door open and Maisy jumped into her arms.

"What do you think you're doing, Harold?" Hate oozed from Juliette's words and her eyes blazed with fire.

"What do you mean, what am *I* doing? I found your poor Maisy running on the beach. Your only responsibility was to keep your eyes on her and you couldn't do that simple task."

Vanessa handed Maisy to Juliette and stepped in front of her so she was close enough to bend down right in Harold's face. "That's a big lie, you bully. Maisy was perfectly happy sitting with that little girl and you snatched her away. Both the girl and Maisy were hysterical."

Harold tried to push Vanessa away. "Butt out, Vanessa. Who asked you to watch over everyone? You stuck to Monique like glue except when it really mattered."

Vanessa's hands clenched into fists.

"That's right. You took your eyes off of your responsibility and look what happened. Monique's death is *your* fault even if you weren't the one to push her in the pool. Now get out of my way. All of you." Harold hissed the words, spewing spittle from his mouth. He wrenched the door closed and started the car.

Juliette hugged Maisy close to her chest. Ruby gently guided her away from Harold's car. Vanessa and Hannah huddled near Ruby and Juliette as Harold sped out of the driveway.

"What a jerk," Vanessa said, more to herself than anyone else as she faced the ocean. "You would think that this beauty would help to offset everything that has gone wrong, but it doesn't," she added under her breath.

Hannah did a double take. "What did you just say?"

"Oh," Vanessa blinked, as if she almost forgot where she was. She flicked her wrist. "It's just a wish I've had for a long time. You know, we're surrounded by so much beauty but then the ugliness of people seeps in and tries to destroy what we hold dear. The beauty helps but it's never enough. Unfortunately." She faced Hannah. "Does that make sense?"

"I think so, *Candace*," Hannah answered, barely whispering the name.

Even behind her sunglasses, Hannah could see the surprise in Vanessa's eyes as she took a few steps away from the others. "How did you know?"

Before Hannah could respond to Vanessa, Samantha holding Petunia's leash, and Jack holding Olivia's hand joined the four women in the parking lot.

Ruby picked up Olivia who was still sniffling. She wiped her eyes with the backs of her little hands. "Is Maisy all right?" Olivia's big eyes filled to overflowing with giant tears.

Juliette turned around so Olivia could see Maisy all snuggled in her arms. "She's fine, Olivia. And are you okay?" Juliette tenderly pushed a few stray hairs out of Olivia's face and tucked them behind her ears.

"Uh-huh," she sniffled. Her hand stroked Maisy's curly hair and the Moodle licked Olivia's hand.

Hannah put her hands out to the sides and herded the group closer to the snack bar. She desperately wanted to figure out a way to talk to Vanessa in private. With everyone talking over each other, it would be a while before she'd be able to get Vanessa away from the others without drawing any attention.

"I can't believe Harold took off like he did," Samantha said. "One minute he was clicking away with his camera—and by the way, Petunia is a natural model—and then he dashed over to the picnic table and scooped up Maisy right out from under Olivia's arm. What an evil, evil man."

"I think I'll take Maisy back to your house if that's okay with you, Ruby. The poor thing is still trembling." Juliette lowered her cheek and rubbed it on Maisy's head.

"That's a good idea. I can put Petunia back in her pen. She's probably ready for another mud bath." Ruby took the leash from Samantha. "Do you want to come with us, too?" she asked Samantha.

"Um," Samantha hesitated. "I think I'll take a rest in my cottage if you don't mind. All of this seems to have drained my energy."

Hannah looked at Jack, hoping he planned to go back to his house. Instead, he asked Hannah, "Do you have anything cold to drink in your cottage? I sure could use a little rehydration after being out in the hot sun with Olivia."

"Sure. How about you, Vanessa? Would you care to join us for a glass of lemonade?" The way Jack had been eyeing Vanessa, Hannah suspected that he had something on his mind to ask her.

"That sounds perfect. I might need something stronger, though," Vanessa replied. "I'll get my bag and join you."

Hannah pointed to the path behind The Fishy Dish that led to her cottage. "We'll be waiting on the porch."

Vanessa slowly walked to her cottage as if her mind was far away from what her body was doing.

"What's going on with Vanessa?" Jack asked Hannah. "You figured something out. Am I right?"

"Yes. It was something written in the guest book that caught my attention." She started walking up the path to her cottage. "I hope Vanessa will finally open up and help us figure out what's going on with Harold."

Hannah decided the situation called for a batch of strawberry daiquiris; not too strong, but with just enough rum to relax Vanessa and loosen her tongue.

CHAPTER 22

Vanessa's sandals slapped on Hannah's porch steps.

"Have a seat and keep me company out here." Jack patted the arm of the Adirondack chair next to him. "It doesn't get much better than watching the waves move in and out, listening to the seagulls squawk overhead, and smell the briny ocean breeze. Hannah's fixing up something to drink."

Vanessa stepped over Nellie who was sprawled out in front of Jack and sat, crossed her legs, and let out a contented sigh.

Jack squinted and studied her face. "You look kind of familiar but I can't figure out from where."

"I stayed in that cottage," Vanessa pointed to Cottage Four, the last cottage, "six years ago."

Jack nodded. "I see." It finally hit him why she looked familiar. "You had brown hair then."

"I did. And it was before a lot of plastic surgery."

"Your name was in the guest book as Candace V. Jones. The V was for Vanessa, wasn't it? You go by Vanessa now."

"I wanted to fly under the radar this time." She jiggled her foot, not offering any more of an explanation.

Hannah arrived with a pitcher and three glasses. She poured a strawberry daiquiri and handed it to Vanessa before she filled the other two glasses for herself and Jack.

She settled into the third chair on the other side of Vanessa and held up her glass. "Cheers."

"How did you figure it out—who I was?" Vanessa asked Hannah.

Hannah looked over her porch railing at the view that she never got tired of seeing. "From what you said after you saved Maisy from Harold, 'this beauty helps to offset everything that has gone wrong'. You wrote the same words in the guest book."

"I forgot about that. I guess those exact thoughts came back when I returned. Along with memories I've tried to run from."

They sat quietly and sipped the drinks before Hannah broke the silence. "Should I call you Candace or Vanessa?"

"I'm Vanessa now. Ever since I left here six years ago. A new name, mostly new face, but the same old scars. They don't show, but you can't easily wipe them away."

"I think you have a lot to share and I'm guessing it will shed some light on what Harold might have done to Monique."

"He can't know who I am." Her fingers tightened on the glass in her hand.

"Are you afraid he might hurt you? Is that what happened six years ago?"

Vanessa set her glass on the wide arm of her chair. "He doesn't scare me anymore but I do worry about the other women he hooks with his smooth lies. At least Juliette escaped. I'm glad about that."

"What happened, Vanessa? Juliette thought you were interested in Harold six years ago and didn't want her to be alone with him." Hannah was trying to wrap her head around this whole Vanessa, Juliette, Harold saga from six years ago.

"I didn't want her to be alone with Harold because I was afraid for *her*."

"Were you trying to protect her six years ago?"

"Yes. And I tried to protect Monique but she had other ideas. She didn't want to believe what I said about Harold, she thought I was jealous or something. But I always travelled with her because I wanted to keep her safe." Vanessa lowered her head.

Jack stared at Vanessa in disbelief. "Did Harold kill Monique?"

"I don't have proof but that's what I think. I could see how he was getting more and more annoyed with Monique. The same thing that happened to me before he bashed my face, paid me off, and bought my silence." She paused. "I'm not proud of that last part, but it is what it is and that's the reason I can't talk about any of this to the police. Harold will sue me and take every last penny I've managed to squirrel away so I can get on with my life."

Jack twisted sideways in his chair so he was facing Vanessa. "Let me get this straight. When you were here with Harold and Juliette six years ago, you tried to protect Juliette but instead, Harold assaulted you and paid you off to keep quiet. Didn't you worry about Juliette when you left?"

"Of course I did." Vanessa scooched forward and twisted her body to face Jack. "I followed every tidbit of information about Harold while I was going through my recovery. When he married Juliette, I had the hope that maybe he changed; maybe he was actually in love with her; maybe he would treat her with respect and dignity." She sipped her drink. "But I still stalked him in every way possible."

"Caroline always thought there was something inherently bad about that guy." Jack settled back in his chair and stared at the ocean. "She wanted to get involved but I told her it was just a lover's spat and to mind her own business."

"Caroline? The owner of the cottages?" Vanessa asked.

"Yes. She—"

"She died and left all this to me." Hannah interrupted before Jack could say too much about Caroline. "Good thing too, Jack, or she'd never let you forget that she was right all along."

"Harrumph. Something tells me I'll still have to pay for my mistake in one way or another."

Hannah caught Jack's eye and she winked at him. Their secret for now.

"Anyway, now we have to figure out what to do about Mr. Harold Chandler III. How to flush him out of the muck. What do you think, Vanessa?" Hannah asked.

"Patience. As long as he's in town, he'll do something stupid. He always does. I only hope he doesn't hurt anyone this time."

"Gwen. Gwen is angling to get in his good graces or in his bed if that's what it takes. She as much as told me that," Hannah said.

Vanessa crossed her legs and seemed to relax. Maybe the rum in the strawberry daiquiri was doing its magic. Or maybe she was just relieved to finally unload some of this burden off her own shoulders. At any rate, she knew the most about what they were dealing with as far as Harold was concerned.

"Gwen is definitely a manipulator. She watched from the edges and undermined Monique every chance she got. You know, like insulting the color of something she was wearing, or pointing out a nonexistent wrinkle or blemish. After a while, all those comments seeped into Harold's subconscious and he turned on Monique."

"Have you warned Gwen?"

"She won't listen. None of them do. Every new girl thinks they'll be the one to snag the charming Mr. Chandler. They hope he'll turn them into a famous model. I know what they think because that's what I thought too, at one time."

Hannah refilled Vanessa's glass. Jack shook his hand indicating he didn't want any more. She topped hers off with the last of the strawberry daiquiri. "Why did you come back here with Monique? Weren't you afraid Harold would recognize you?"

"It crossed my mind but my hair is blonde now and my face is different enough from when he saw me six years ago. I've put on enough weight that he wouldn't see me as swimsuit model material and if I have no use to him, I assumed I would become invisible in Harold's world. The thing is, Monique is a close friend. I couldn't talk her out of working for Harold so I decided all I could hope for was to stay with her so I could keep an eye on her and protect her." Vanessa's hands covered her face. "I failed."

Hannah reached out to comfort Vanessa. "You did what you could. In the end, Monique is responsible for her choices."

"I suppose so, but it doesn't make it any easier to accept her death. Such a senseless end to a beautiful person."

"Speak of the devil," Jack said, his eyes on the bright red car that just pulled into the parking lot. "It looks like Harold has returned."

Hannah stood and moved to her porch railing. "Gwen is waving and running over to meet him. That won't sit well with Colin. I heard him say he'd be back to pick her up to take her out for dinner."

"Figures," Vanessa said. Her voice was sounding a bit slurred. "She'll chase after whoever she thinks will help her the most at the moment. Poor Colin won't have a chance if Gwen has her claws out for Harold."

"There they go. Gwen just climbed into Harold's car. Do you think she's safe with him?" Hannah leaned as far forward as possible over her porch railing to get a better view into Harold's car.

Vanessa flicked her wrist dismissively. "There's no other competition for her at the moment so Harold will probably turn his charm on. She'll think she's got him wrapped around her finger but it's Harold who has Gwen snared in his web. That's how he works. Once he zeroes in on a new model, Gwen better get out while she has the chance."

Hannah had her phone out and to her ear. "Samantha? Meet me in the office as soon as possible. I need some help." She slid her phone back in her pocket. "Vanessa, are you okay for the rest of the day? I've got some errands to run."

Jack raised his eyebrows questionably in Hannah's direction. He never missed much.

Vanessa pushed herself out of the Adirondack chair. She reached for the porch railing to steady herself. "I'll be fine. Just point me in the right direction." She giggled. "I'm ready to sit on my cottage porch and watch the world go by."

With Jack and Hannah each holding one of Vanessa's arms, the three walked down the path. Jack escorted Vanessa all the way to her cottage while Hannah detoured to her office.

By the time Jack returned, Samantha entered from her half of the cottage, looking well-rested. Her eyes danced with expectation of something exciting. She rubbed her hands together. "Don't keep me in suspense. What's the plan?"

"Gwen just blew Colin off for his dinner date with her. I think it's time to grill him on what he knows about her whereabouts when Monique got pushed in the pool. He has his eye on Gwen but, hopefully, he's not stupid enough to lie for her."

"Gwen is the murderer?" Samantha asked with far too much excitement in her voice.

"I think it has to be Gwen or Harold and the two of them are together at the moment which we can use to our advantage with Colin."

"What about Juliette?"

"Or Juliette, I suppose, although I don't want that to be the case." Hannah walked out of the office.

"I'll drive," Samantha said. She pointed her key fob at her royal blue Mini Cooper. The car beeped and the lights flickered on and off.

"Drop me at my house? You didn't invite me along on your adventure so I'll just sit at home by myself." Jack pouted.

"Do you want to come?" Hannah asked.

Jack grinned. "Thanks for the invitation." He climbed in the back seat and buckled himself in. "That poor boy has no idea what's about to hit him when the two of you get him cornered."

CHAPTER 23

As Samantha drove to the Paradise Inn, Hannah told her what Vanessa revealed about Harold and how he had assaulted her.

"That piece of scum. He assaulted her and she needed plastic surgery? I can't believe it." Samantha took the corner a little too fast and her wheels squealed.

Hannah put her hands on the dash to steady herself. "Slow down, Mario. We aren't in a race. I checked with Ruby, and Colin is working tonight. She said we'd probably find him out back taking his break."

Samantha swerved into a parking spot, barely missing the fender of the car she parked next to.

"That was close," Hannah said as she carefully opened her door. There was barely enough room for her to squeeze out without bashing her door into the other car.

"I think that other driver is over the line into my parking spot. I hope he doesn't hit me when he backs out." Samantha slammed her door and headed to the entrance of the Paradise Inn.

Jack and Hannah exchanged a look. She cupped her hand around her mouth. "Remind me to never park near Samantha."

Jack nodded in agreement.

"Samantha!" Hannah called. "I'm going to walk around to the back on the outside of the building instead of going inside."

Samantha stopped at the fountain and reversed her direction. "Should we split up in case he tries to make a run for it?"

"Why would he do that? We only want to talk to him."

"Oh, right." Samantha clearly sounded disappointed.

Jack dawdled behind them but that was okay with Hannah. If they came on too strong, Colin might get spooked and be less inclined to give them information. She certainly didn't want him to be on the defensive. "Let me do the talking, Samantha." In other words, please keep your mouth zipped up tight.

"Why did you bring me along if I can't say anything?"

"I need another set of ears. You can charm him if you want, but try not to accuse him of murdering Monique."

"I can do charm." Samantha swiveled her hips and patted her curls. "Harold complimented my modeling this afternoon, by the way. I think I'm a natural."

"Well, if I were you, I wouldn't turn my back on that guy." Hannah spotted Colin sitting by himself at a picnic table. She made a beeline in his direction.

"Hey, Colin. Do you have a minute?" Hannah stuck her hand in the air to get his attention.

He looked up and grinned. "Sure, about five more, to be exact. Management is pretty strict that we don't stretch it out. But it's a decent job. What's up?"

"Not much. Actually, I'm surprised to find you here," she lied. "I thought I heard you tell Gwen that you would be picking her up to take her to dinner. Bummer that work got in the way." Hannah sat next to Colin to be at his eye level instead of looking down at him.

"Actually, she called me and said she wasn't feeling good so I switched with someone who wanted tonight off. I'm hoping she'll be better by tomorrow night when I get off work." He fiddled with his phone, checking his Facebook feed from what Hannah could see from the corner of her eye.

"Sick? That's a shame. I'm sure I saw Harold pick her up." Hannah shrugged. "Maybe he was taking her to the doctor or something."

"Huh? All she had was a headache. Why would she go to the doctor for that?"

"She blew you off," Samantha said. She obviously ran out of patience to keep her lips zipped. She sat next to Hannah, shoved her with her hips to make more room, and leaned forward to see Colin better. "Don't you get it? She's playing you for a fool. Believe me, I've been around long enough to know what *I have a headache* means."

Hannah jabbed Samantha's side to get her to shut up. It didn't work. "I'm sure she has a good explanation."

Colin's face lost its goofy grin. "I can't believe it. She lied to me?"

Samantha patted his leg. "Looks like it, dear. What are you going to do about it?"

Colin stood and paced back and forth. "I'll tell you what I'm *not* going to do. I'm not going to lie for her. I promised I'd go to the police station when I got off work and tell Deputy Larson that I was with Gwen when she was on her break. The security camera back there doesn't work so no one would know if I lied."

"Except you," Jack said. He leaned against the neighboring picnic table with his arms crossed. "And when you lie to the police, and they find out, they don't like it too much."

"What will I tell Gwen? She's going to be mad at me if I don't do this." Colin looked at Jack, then Hannah, then Samantha.

Samantha stood next to Colin with her hands on his arms. She stared into his eyes. "Listen, dear, you don't want to ruin your life over someone as shallow as Gwen appears to be. I can tell you're a hardworking and good looking," she winked at Colin, "young man."

"I've got an idea, Colin," Hannah said before Samantha got out of control. "Don't tell Gwen anything. She'll assume you will do what you said and leave it at that. Let me ask you this."

Colin nodded.

"Why do you think she wants you to lie for her? I wonder," Hannah paused, "is it possible that Gwen followed Monique into the pool area and pushed her in?" Hannah tried to make it sound like she just this minute got the idea that Gwen could be the killer. She wanted to plant the idea in his head if he hadn't considered it yet. Could he really be that blind, she wondered?

"Gwen?" Colin's eyes darted from Hannah back to Samantha. "Gwen's not a murderer, is she?" he whispered.

"Listen, Colin, you should probably stay clear of her until the police get to the bottom of this." Hannah put her hand on his shoulder. "You don't want to be connected to the murder in case, you know, she *is* involved, do you?"

"I...um...need to get back to work." He jogged back inside as if something was after him and the building would provide a safety net.

"That boy has it bad for Gwen," Jack said. "I hope he has enough sense to take your advice, but I wouldn't put money on him making the right choice. He's young and he has stars in his eyes when it comes to Gwen."

"He won't do anything until he's off work, so we have some time to get more answers." Hannah started walking back toward Samantha's car. "It's time to have another chat with Juliette. She said she scheduled the photoshoot in Hooks Harbor because of unfinished business. It's time she gives us the details about what that unfinished business is."

Samantha zipped her Mini Cooper out of the parking spot, narrowly missing side-swiping the car she almost hit on the way into the spot. Hannah sighed with relief. Time for dealing with a parking lot fender-bender was not scheduled into her day.

"What is your latest theory about this mess, Hannah?" Jack

asked from the backseat. "If these suspects have shared even half what they've told you, Pam must be pulling her hair out."

"Now that we know more about Vanessa and all that she told us about Harold, I still think he's the top suspect." She turned around as much as possible to face Jack. "Harold assaulted Vanessa. He dumped Juliette. He argued with Monique and, if everything is true, she was driving him crazy. Harold does *not* have any patience."

Samantha drove into Hannah's parking lot, stirring up a cloud of dust.

When Samantha was safely stopped, Hannah continued. "And here's why I think Harold is the likely murderer. With Juliette's terrible fight with Monique over the dog-napping fiasco, and Juliette in the pool area when Monique went missing, Harold has the perfect person to pin the blame on."

Samantha put her elbow on the back of her seat so she could see both Hannah and Jack. "The way I see it, if Vanessa comes forward with her information about Harold, Pam will have to give him a good close look. Monique's death fits right into his abusive pattern toward women."

"And that's a problem because Vanessa won't go to the police. She may have signed a confidentiality agreement or something like that when Harold paid her off." Hannah opened her door. "I'm going to get the dogs and head to Ruby's house. If Juliette can remember more details from when she stayed here six years ago, maybe she can be her own best defense since there's still a lot of circumstantial evidence pointing right at her."

"Or she's a good liar," Jack said.

"That is a possibility. I don't know her very well but I want to trust Ruby's sense about Juliette."

Nellie and Patches were sprawled on Hannah's porch. Nellie got up and greeted her with a fiercely wagging tail but Patches only managed to raise his head up and howl. "That's ok, Patches, don't get up on my account." Hannah laughed and reached down to scratch behind his ears. "You do know how to get comfy, I have to give you that."

Her screen door opened from the inside and surprised her.

"Well, look what the wind finally blew home."

Hannah smiled when she saw Cal's twinkling eyes. "Have you been here for long?" This was an unexpected but wonderful surprise.

"Not too long. I stopped by to show you something I made. It's inside."

Hannah's stomach growled. Cal didn't have a large repertoire of cooking specialties, but right about now, anything would satisfy her stomach. She followed him inside and sniffed the air. Her eyes looked at the empty kitchen table. "You didn't bring food?"

"It's in your fridge. I still need to cook it, but that's not what I want you to see." He pointed to a wooden box about the size of a rectangular baking pan placed exactly in the middle of her coffee table.

The cherry wood was buffed to a deep glassy sheen. Hannah mouthed the letters—O L I V I A—engraved in the top. She looked at Cal. "It's beautiful. Olivia will be ecstatic, but…"

Cal's face fell. "No buts, Hannah. I spent hours on this. Don't tell me there's something wrong." He picked up the box. "Did I spell her name wrong?"

Hannah laughed. "No, nothing like that. It just might be a tad too small. Olivia gathers more shells, rocks, and colorful sea glass every time we take a walk on the beach."

"That sounds more like it's Ruby's problem. She may have to put an addition on her house with shelves just for Olivia's collections."

"And there's one other problem. Olivia said you were making her a box with a lock."

Cal handed the box to Hannah. "I didn't forget. I can add a

lock but I'm not sure she really needs to lock up her treasures yet. If she loses the key, she'll be one very unhappy little girl."

"Good point. I think she'll be so happy with the box, she'll forget all about whether it locks or not. Let's call Ruby and tell them to come over to see it."

Hannah heard feet stomping on her porch steps. "You already called, didn't you?"

"I couldn't wait. And I have enough food for everyone as long as burgers are good enough."

Olivia burst through Hannah's door, followed by Maisy and Nellie who managed to push in front of Ruby and Juliette. Patches decided to stay on the porch.

Cal held the box hidden behind his back. Olivia moved in a slow circle, her eyes wide and her mouth open. "Mom said there was a surprise here for me, but I don't see anything." Her tiny voice was filled with sadness.

Hannah picked up her niece. "Aren't I a nice surprise? And Cal?" She twirled around so they faced him.

He held one empty hand in front.

"What's in your other hand, Cal?"

He moved his empty hand behind his back and showed her his other hand which was now empty.

Olivia's mouth turned down and her bottom lip puffed out. "I was hoping you had my new treasure box."

Cal slowly revealed the new cherry box from behind his back.

Olivia's eyes grew.

She reached her hands out.

Hannah put her down and Olivia carried the beautiful box to the table. She lifted the lid. The inside was lined with pink velvet. She looked at Cal. "It's exactly what I wanted. How did you know?"

Cal sat cross-legged on the floor next to Olivia. She flopped into his lap. "Because you drew a picture of what you wanted, you silly. Do you think you have enough treasures to fill it up?" Cal caught Hannah's eye.

"Only my favorite and most specialist colored glass and shells will go in this box. My rocks will stay in my old box." She rubbed the velvet with her fingers. "It's as soft as Nellie's ears."

"I'm glad you love it, Olivia."

She turned her face toward Cal's. "As soon as I get home, I'll show it to Theodore. He's going to love it, too."

While Olivia chatted to Cal about what she and Theodore had been doing, Ruby pulled Hannah off to one side. "I got a call from work. Colin never returned after his break."

This news made no sense to Hannah. "I talked to him while he was on his break and he went back inside when we were done."

"Well, he may have gone inside, but he walked right out the front door and left."

"What does this mean?" Hannah asked.

"I don't know. What did you say to him?"

"I told him that I saw Gwen get in Harold's car and he shouldn't go to the police and lie for her."

"He didn't go to the police. No one seems to know where he is."

"Maybe *he* pushed Monique into the pool and needed Gwen to be *his* alibi." Hannah couldn't believe the words that came out of her mouth. She hadn't seen this coming.

CHAPTER 24

The fog that hung over Hannah's cottage on Tuesday morning made her want to pull the pillow over her face and stay in bed.

But Nellie whined to go out.

"Okay. I'll get up," she said to the dogs. "But, if it weren't for the two of you, I think I'd just call in sick today."

It was more than the fog that made her want to skip the day, it was all the swirling information in her head surrounding Monique's murder. When one clue seemed to point toward one person, another tidbit would by revealed to muddy the path—Juliette fighting with Monique about the dog-napping, Harold wanting Monique out of his life, Gwen wanting to be the top model and Harold's latest trophy girlfriend, and now, Colin disappearing which could mean nothing or it could mean he was trying to help Gwen get what *she* wanted so he could have *her*.

Hannah shook her head and tried to dislodge the webs.

Without any luck.

What was she missing?

Hannah skipped her morning coffee and, instead, she slipped on her flip-flops and took the dogs for an earlier than usual walk on the beach. They didn't mind in the least. They still had seagulls to bark at and waves to chase. What could be more fun than that for a couple of dogs?

Hannah only had too much to think about.

As a figure approached through the fog, she silently groaned. Having the beach to herself first thing in the morning gave her the chance to organize her day without interruption. But now an interruption was quickly approaching.

"Good morning, Hannah," Vanessa called. "I didn't expect to bump into anyone this early."

Hannah stopped and bent down to pick up a polished piece of sea glass to surprise Olivia with when she saw her.

"I had an interesting chat with Harold last night."

At the mention of Harold's name, Hannah's ears perked up. "Oh?"

Vanessa crossed her arms and looked down at the sand. "I couldn't believe it, but he opened up to me. It might have had something to do with too many drinks on his part, but in any case, he talked a lot about Monique."

Hannah rubbed the sea glass between her fingers, trying to be patient.

"He actually apologized to me for saying her death was my fault and he even accepted part of the blame." Vanessa looked at Hannah. "He thinks that if he hadn't pushed her to learn to swim, maybe she wouldn't have gone near the pool. He wasn't mad at her like I thought, but he said being back here was distracting for him. Without going into details, he said he had regrets from his past."

"Huh. And he still doesn't recognize you as the model he assaulted all those years ago?"

Vanessa turned to face the ocean. She inhaled and let out a long, deep breath of air. "I don't think so. I wanted to tell him. To comfort him. Tell him we've all made mistakes, but…I couldn't get the words out."

What was it with these models? As soon as Harold turned on his charm, they seemed to melt in front of him. "What do you make of all that? Was he sincere or only trying to cover himself as a suspect?"

Vanessa's hand darted out and rested on Hannah's arm. "Oh no. It came from his heart. He also said his biggest mistake was cheating on Juliette, not that he didn't care deeply for Monique," she added quickly. Her voice got hard. "He said he still loves Juliette."

Hannah didn't miss the change in Vanessa's voice. "And that doesn't sit well with you?"

"I guess it doesn't. I thought Harold was incapable of love."

The dogs ran circles around Hannah. They were getting impatient for her to continue their walk. "What about Gwen? How does she fit into all of this?"

Vanessa's eyebrows furrowed into a scowl. "She has always been after Harold. I hope the police are looking into *her* whereabouts when Monique went missing."

"I saw her get into Harold's car late yesterday afternoon. When did *you* bump into him to talk to him?" Apparently, Harold had a busy evening.

She waved her hand away as if the thought of Harold and Gwen together was nothing more than an annoying gnat. "She called him to give her a ride back to the Paradise Inn. I was eating at the Inn restaurant when he saw me." She laughed.

"That had to be an awkward moment."

"I couldn't believe it when he sat down across from me. I almost told him to leave." She shrugged. "But I decided it couldn't hurt to hear what he had to say. And I was lonely. I wanted someone to talk to about Monique. Someone who had also been close to her."

Hannah couldn't help but wonder where Gwen was now. Was she with Colin? If she went back to the Inn, did she corner Colin into taking her somewhere after all?

"How long are you planning to stay around?" Hannah asked.

"Oh, until this is resolved. I need to have closure and," she lowered her voice even though they were the only ones on the beach, "I'm hoping Gwen gets arrested for Monique's murder."

"Not Harold?" Hannah thought Vanessa wanted revenge for what Harold did to her all those years ago.

She shrugged. "I guess I've forgiven him. I know, it sounds crazy and I can't believe it myself, but life is too short to hold a grudge."

Hannah watched Vanessa as she continued toward the cottages. That was the biggest turnaround she could remember. Maybe Harold had a charming side but it was nothing that *she* had seen evidence of. Or maybe all these women who were attracted to him had a little bit of crazy in their personality. Hannah suspected it was the latter.

Nellie and Patches raced down the beach, happy to be moving again. They cut through the path that led through the boulders across from Jack's house.

Was it too early to pop in for coffee?

Pam's car was in the driveway so Hannah knew Jack would be up and the coffee would be hot. She let herself in.

"Open the letter, Dad." Hannah heard Pam's angry voice coming from the kitchen.

"Is the coffee hot?" Hannah called so as to give them time to know she was in the house.

"You are just in time, Hannah," Jack said. Hannah thought there was more to his words than being in time for coffee. He was probably also happy that she came when she did so Pam would get off his back about the medical lab results.

Pam glared at Hannah. "Maybe *you* can talk some sense into this stubborn old man. He certainly won't listen to me. I have to find a couple of missing persons." She stomped to the door, slamming it on her way out.

"Ouch." Hannah accepted a steaming mug of coffee from Jack. "I guess you haven't opened the letter yet."

"And why is my health anyone's business but my own?"

Hannah bit her tongue. It wouldn't help to tell Jack that of course, his health was important to everyone who loved him, especially his daughter. He would have to figure it out in his own time. She switched to a marginally safer topic. "Is Pam looking for Colin who works at the Paradise Inn, by any chance?"

"How do you know about Colin?"

"Ruby told me. He left work yesterday and no one knows where he is. Who else is missing?"

"The other model. Apparently, when the maid service went in to clean her room, all her stuff was gone but she never checked out or paid her bill."

"Does Pam think they are missing together?" That certainly seemed to be a strong possibility as far as Hannah was concerned. Colin was obviously smitten with Gwen, and Gwen could use him to her advantage if need be.

"She didn't come out and say it, but reading between the lines, it's my assumption."

Hannah sipped her coffee and frowned. "Your coffee is a little off this morning. What happened?" As a matter of fact, his coffee matched his mood.

Jack glared at her. "Make your own coffee. Beggars can't be choosy. Now, get out of here, I have things to do." He flicked his wrist back and forth as if the motion would sweep her right out the door.

Hannah got the hint. She knew better than to stay around Jack when he would rather be miserable by himself. Geesh. If he didn't hurry up and look at his lab results, she'd do it for him to get him over his anxiety.

"Come on you two. At least you're always happy to see me." Hannah patted both dogs and turned toward Ruby's house, glad to see that the fog was lifting.

When Hannah walked inside, Olivia was sitting on the floor in the living room with her new treasure box open in front of her. Maisy sat on one side of her and Theodore was propped against a chair on the other side.

"And this is blue sea glass. I think blue is my favorite color because it matches the sky and the ocean and Cal's eyes. Cal has nice eyes," she explained to Maisy and Theodore.

Hannah smiled. She had to agree with Olivia about Cal's eyes—blue, kind, and sexy. "I found something for your treasure box, if you still have room?"

Olivia whipped her head around. "Well, it has to be really, really special to get a spot in my new treasure box, Aunt Hannah."

Hannah dug in her pocket and handed Olivia the sea glass she found on the beach. She held her breath as Olivia turned it over in her hand and examined it. Would it make the cut?

"It's beautiful. I'll put it right here next to this piece that Cal gave me. You and Cal go together so your sea glass should go together, too."

Hannah's hand pressed against her heart. How did this little girl get to be so insightful? She sat on the floor next to Olivia. "Can I see what else you have in there?"

"Sure." Olivia proceeded to point to each treasure and explain where it came from and who gave it to her and why it was special. Every piece had a story connected to the ocean or the beach which made Hannah's heart sing with happiness.

When Olivia finished, Hannah asked, "Where's your mom?"

"In the kitchen talking to Juliette. They didn't want me to listen, but I'm really not interested in that grown up talk about modeling stuff. I never want to be a model. I want to be like you, Aunt Hannah. I want to help you run your business when I grow up. I want to dress in shorts and flip-flops and eat all the ice cream I want."

Hannah stared at her niece and blinked back the tears of joy that she felt filling up her eyes. She was too choked up to say anything so she patted Olivia's head before she walked into the kitchen.

"How can you even think about going back to Harold? He cheated on you, Juliette." Ruby shook her head with disgust.

Juliette sat quietly with her head down.

"Hannah? Talk some sense into her if you can."

Hannah sat at the table across from Juliette. Today must be the day that everyone thought she could talk sense into someone else. First, Pam wanted her to talk sense into Jack and now she was supposed to talk sense into Juliette. She wondered why everyone else thought she possessed some sort of special power to convince someone else to change their mind about a decision. Maybe the secret was, if she just let the other person talk and she listened, they eventually solved the problem in their own time.

"I'm wondering about one thing, Juliette. What happened six years ago between Harold and Candace?" Hannah asked.

"I told you. She had an argument with Harold and she left."

"Did he assault her?"

Juliette's eyes widened in shock. "Assault? Not that I'm aware of. I saw her get in her car and leave. She left me a nasty note at the time but I burned it. I didn't want any memory of her or the horrible things she said to me."

"You must remember the gist of the note."

Ruby filled a mug with coffee and set it down in front of Hannah. She hoped this was better than Jack's coffee since she'd only taken one sip of that horrible bitter brew.

Juliette sighed. "It said something about how I had ruined her chances with Harold and she hoped I had the same fate. There was also a lot of criticism of my figure, my modeling, my...you name it. That's what I've blocked out. I found the note stuffed in my bikini top after she was gone. My bikini top that she cut in half."

Hannah's eyebrows shot up and her jaw dropped. "That sounds like she had some anger issues." She got up the nerve to try

Ruby's coffee which usually was weak. It was, but at least it wasn't bitter. "Did you tell Harold about it?"

"No. Why bother? She left and Harold turned on his charm. We were married within the year."

Ruby peeked around the kitchen door. "Olivia is completely engrossed with the new treasure box from Cal. I think he'll be her favorite person forever."

"I gave her a new piece of sea glass and she had to do a thorough inspection before she decided it could have a place of honor next to a piece of sea glass that Cal gave her." Hannah didn't tell Ruby about the rest of her conversation about what she wanted to do when she grew up, she'd save that for when Juliette was gone.

Hannah tapped her fingernails on the table and brought her attention back to Juliette. "Something doesn't add up." Vanessa told Hannah a very different story about why she left.

"She was furious that she got dumped," Juliette said. "Now I know how she feels since it happened to me when Gwen got hired, just like Candace predicted."

Hannah let the conversation taper off. Juliette had her version and Vanessa had hers. Someone was lying. Or not, since there was a good possibility that the assault was kept hidden from Juliette. She might have to try and have a conversation with Harold. But what was the chance he'd admit to assaulting Vanessa when he knew her as Candace?

CHAPTER 25

Jack was busy chatting and sampling Meg's latest pastry creations when Hannah finally got herself back to The Fishy Dish kitchen.

And he was in a *good* mood.

A tray filled with lemon scones, dainty strawberry tarts, and slices of chocolate chip banana bread sat on the counter.

Hannah reached her hand toward the tray.

Meg slapped it away before Hannah even got close. "Close your eyes and I'll let you have a bite of something."

Hannah closed her eyes and opened her mouth. The aroma overwhelming her nose made her salivary glands work overtime. Nothing touched her lips. She opened one eye and took a peek.

Hannah and Jack were both laughing. "Here. Feed yourself," Meg said. "Try the strawberry tart first. I think it's my best creation yet."

Hannah didn't need to be told twice. She nibbled on the edge. The crust was rich and flakey. A thin sweet cream cheese layer covered the crust and made a bed for the thinly sliced strawberries. Her eyes rolled skyward as she inhaled a bigger bite. "This is like a taste of heaven, Meg."

Meg beamed with pleasure. "I thought you'd like it. It's a favorite of one of your guests, too."

Hannah stopped chewing. "Which one?" she mumbled through a mouthful of deliciousness.

"Harold Chandler the la-di-da-Third," Meg twirled her finger in the air as she said Harold's name. "He's been sitting at that picnic table for the last half hour. Didn't you see him when you got here?"

"I did and I detoured around the back."

"Well, you'd better get out there before he eats everything I've made for the guests. He's already helped himself to a half dozen of the tarts." She handed Hannah a pot of coffee. "Fill him up with this instead of any more of my hard work."

Hannah took the coffee pot, straightened her shoulders, and told herself to not let Harold intimidate her. "More coffee?" she asked in her best, you-are-the-customer voice she could manage.

Harold held his mug up but kept his eyes focused on the horizon. "It wasn't supposed to end this way."

"Excuse me?"

"My swimsuit shoot. It wasn't supposed to end the way it did," Harold repeated.

"Well, of course not. I can't imagine you planned to have your model drown in the pool at the Paradise Inn." Or maybe he did but hoped it would look like an accident.

He turned his head and looked at Hannah. "I'm not sure everyone would agree with you about that, but thanks for the vote of confidence." His gaze returned to the horizon.

Hannah sat next to Harold. "Can I ask you about your visit with Gwen last night?"

"Huh? What are you talking about?"

"Don't play cute, Harold. I saw her get in your fancy bright red Alpha Romeo. It's not exactly a car that flies under the radar."

"She needed a ride to the Paradise Inn." He shrugged. "There's no law against that. Besides, she's working for me and I wanted to help her."

"So you know where she is now?"

"She's an adult. I don't keep tabs on her. I told her I wouldn't be doing any more photos until this is all sorted out with Monique. I just can't get myself to concentrate."

Hannah could understand that problem since he was probably distracted worrying about whether he'd be arrested or not. Maybe that was also why he had to stuff himself with Meg's delicious strawberry tarts. "She's missing and you're the last person to be seen with her." Hannah had no idea if that was true or not, but it was worth a bluff.

Harold's face blanched. "What are you talking about?"

"Gwen and an employee from the Inn are both missing. I don't know if they are together or not. I was hoping you might be able to shed some light on the whereabouts of *your employee*."

Harold stood. His mug of coffee was untouched but there were plenty of crumbs as evidence of his indulgence of Meg's pastries. "I don't know anything about where she is." He started to walk away.

"What about Vanessa?" Hannah asked to Harold's back.

"I'm done answering your questions. Go bother someone else." She watched as he walked to his cottage and went inside. At least he wouldn't be eating any more of Meg's strawberry tarts.

Hannah went into the office side of cottage one, *Run on Inn*, and closed the door. The warm glow of Great Aunt Caroline's old oak desk, covered with years of scars, was always a relaxing influence.

What would Great Aunt Caroline do about all the conflicts surrounding Hannah? Probably confront Harold about assaulting Candace six years ago, tell Jack to get over himself and look at the darn lab report, and force Juliette to finalize her divorce so she and Maisy could move on with their lives.

But Hannah wasn't Caroline and her style was so much less confrontational.

While she daydreamed in her office chair with her ankles crossed, resting on the desk, the phone rang, blasting away any chance for peace and quiet.

"Holiday Hideaway Cottages," she answered. "Hannah speaking, how can I help you?"

All she heard was breathing and was about to hang up but a whispery voice came through the phone line. "I need help."

"Who is this?" Hannah asked.

"Gwen. I'm scared."

Hannah's feet crashed to the floor and she lurched up straight. "Where are you, Gwen? What's wrong?"

"I can't talk for long. Colin went outside and he told me not to tell anyone where I am." Gwen's voice was barely audible to Hannah.

"Are you in danger?"

"I...I don't know. He told me I wasn't safe at the Inn and he could hide me but I had to do exactly what he said."

"Tell me where you are, Gwen," Hannah said with as much authority as she could add to her voice without sounding panicked.

"A cottage, not too far from the Inn...maybe a ten or fifteen minute drive. Past a marina. I remember seeing that sign and thinking how much fun it would be to go on a boat."

"Can you remember any more details?"

"Colin drove us here in his black mustang." There was a long pause. "He's coming back inside."

The phone went dead against Hannah's ear.

Hannah's heart hammered. Did Colin push Monique into the pool for some twisted reason to get close to Gwen? Or did Colin know something and he thought he was actually protecting her from the real killer? But what could he know? Hannah stood.

Maybe he had a run-in with Harold and decided *he* was a threat to Gwen.

Without stopping to think of a good strategy, Hannah picked up Great Aunt Caroline's guest sign-in book from six years earlier and left her office in the direction of Harold's cottage. He admitted that he gave Gwen a ride to the Paradise Inn and Colin could have seen them. It was very possible that Colin had some sort of confrontation with Harold.

As she walked, she called Pam and gave her the little bit of information that Gwen had shared. "Try to find her, Pam. She sounded desperate."

"I'm on my way," Pam answered before she hung up.

Hannah looked up as Vanessa headed in her direction. "You look like the world just fell out from under your feet," Vanessa said.

Hannah forced herself to relax and pasted on a friendly smile. "I've got a lot on my mind at the moment. Where are *you* off to?"

"Another walk on the beach. I have a few things to sort out and the beach does wonders for my thought process."

"Nothing better," Hannah said over her shoulder as she kept walking past Vanessa to Harold's cottage.

She knocked and tapped her foot impatiently. What if he'd already left?

The door opened.

"What do you want? More of your questions?"

Hannah slid her foot into the door opening so Harold wouldn't be able to slam it in her face. He could slam it on her foot which would hurt like heck, though, she realized since she only had flip-flops to protect the bottom of her feet. She mustered up some courage. "I do have a question, Harold." She held the book up.

His eyes opened wider than normal and his lips squished into a tight line. "Come in."

"No. Let's sit out here." Hannah pointed to the chairs on the small porch attached to the cottage. The last thing she wanted was to be stuck inside with a possible murderer.

Harold grabbed her arm and pulled her inside the cottage, slamming the door and keeping his body between the only escape from the cottage and Hannah. It all happened in the blink of an eye and she didn't have time to react. She wiped the sweaty palm of her free hand on her shorts and clutched the guest book to her chest.

Harold wrenched the book from her hand.

"What is in that book that has you on edge?" Hannah found her voice, shaky but functional. She was stuck in this mess so she had better use all her ammunition to end it.

Harold opened the book to the page where the marker stuck out. He ripped it from the binding and crumpled it into a tiny ball. "There, now it's not a problem anymore."

"You can throw the page away, but how will you hide *Candace V. Jones*? That is the name of the other model, isn't it?" Hannah stepped closer to Harold. "You paid her off, didn't you?"

"You don't know what you're talking about. You have no idea what happened here six years ago." Harold held Hannah's gaze like a predator trying to paralyze its prey with fear.

She forced herself to take another step closer. "Why don't you tell me what happened?"

"No. It was between Candace and me and *she'll* never talk, I made sure of that."

If Hannah didn't know that Candace was alive and well, masquerading as Vanessa now, she would have to wonder if Harold's comment meant he killed her. "How much money did you give her?"

"Enough so she could disappear. That's what she wanted."

"Disappear? From you?"

His brows scrunched together. "That was the deal. She would disappear and never bother me again. Never stalk me. Never threaten anyone close to me. Why do you insist on opening up those old wounds? Did Juliette put you up to this? It would be just like her to spite me like that."

"No. Juliette only said that you and Candace argued and then Candace left. What was the argument about?"

Harold sighed. His body deflated. "Juliette. Candace hated her. For some reason, Candace thought *she* should be the only model in my life. She was my worst nightmare."

"Juliette was the reason she left?"

"I suppose, in a way, everything came to a head because of Juliette, and I was trying to protect her from Candace's wrath. Talk to Juliette. She knows the truth about Candace."

Something was wrong with this picture. Was Candace protecting Juliette from Harold six years ago like she told Hannah, or was it the other way around? "And you and Juliette got married soon after Candace disappeared?"

"Yes. Everything was wonderful, until—"

"Monique came into the picture."

Harold nodded.

"You have a habit of getting women out of your life, don't you?" She ticked names off on her fingers. "Candace, Juliette, and now Monique. How easy for you to give Monique a nudge with your elbow and watch her sink to the bottom of the pool so you could move on to Gwen. Did Colin figure out your plan?"

Harold's jaw dropped. "Who is Colin?"

"He works at the Paradise Inn. He was supposed to take Gwen to dinner last night but she went with you instead. Did he confront you?" Hannah sidestepped to get a clear path to the door.

"He drives a mustang?"

Hannah nodded.

"I saw him leave with Gwen after I dropped her off. And listen," his eyes blazed with anger, "I didn't push Monique into the pool. I don't know where you got that idea from. I was getting my lights and equipment ready to start the photoshoot. The police have checked and rechecked and triple checked my alibi and they said I'm off the suspect list. I'm only sticking around until the police figure this out."

It was Hannah's turn to be shocked.

"Here's another tidbit for you," Harold said. "Colin works at the Inn?"

Hannah nodded.

"The police told me the security cameras had been tampered with. Maybe you should be sticking your nose into *Colin's* business. *He* could have followed Monique into the pool area and pushed her in," Harold said. "If Gwen is with him now, she could be in danger." He grabbed Hannah's arm. "Help me find her."

Hannah's arm tingled. Could she trust this man? Everything about him screamed for her to run as fast as possible away from him.

Hannah forced herself to act calm even though every nerve burned as adrenaline surged through her body. Her focus was to get out of the cottage where, at least, she could make a run for safety if necessary.

CHAPTER 26

Hannah had never been so happy to see Samantha rushing toward her as she walked next to Harold. She didn't know why, but just being within inches of him made her muscles twitch.

Samantha grinned broadly and primped her hair when she caught sight of Harold. "Petunia escaped again. Can you help me catch her, Hannah? We could do some more photos if you want, Harold."

Hannah shook her head, trying to discourage Samantha from getting too cozy with him. All she needed added to her plate was to rescue Samantha from Harold's clutches. "He's busy. But I'll help you, Samantha. Let's go."

She felt fingers grip her arm and she almost let out a scream.

"You didn't tell me where Gwen is," Harold said.

"Look for Colin's black Mustang somewhere past the marina. That's all I know."

Hannah sighed a huge sigh of relief when Harold released her arm and walked to his car.

"What was *that* all about?" Samantha asked.

"I'm not sure yet but I'm glad to be away from him. Where is Petunia?"

"She was begging at The Fishy Dish back door but as soon as I tried to get her, she squealed and took off for your cottage. Maybe she wants to hang out with the dogs."

"I've got popcorn inside I can use for a treat. That's her favorite." Hannah and Samantha quickly walked toward Hannah's cottage. When Petunia spotted them, she trotted around to the back but Nellie and Patches rushed toward Hannah. "Stay here with Samantha and I'll get you some treats, too," she promised the dogs.

Nellie sat at the word treat and waited patiently. Patches wasn't sure but, in the end, he decided to stay with Nellie and Samantha. "I'll be right back," Hannah told them.

With a bowl of popcorn and a handful of dog bones, Hannah returned outside. "Let's ignore Petunia for now. I think she'll get curious once she smells food and she'll head in our direction."

Sure enough, as Nellie and Patches munched their dog bones, and Hannah scattered some popcorn on the ground, Petunia casually made her appearance with her nose in the air, trotted over to the popcorn trail, and cleaned up the pieces. She looked expectantly at Hannah as if to say, *that's all?*

"You want more, do you?" Hannah held the bowl between herself and Samantha. "When she sticks her head in the bowl, wrap the leash around her. I think the popcorn will distract her enough so we can get her harness on."

The plan went without a hitch. "I guess it's best if I bring her back to her pen before she gets into any real trouble."

"I'll come too," Samantha offered.

Of course, Nellie and Patches led the way.

Ruby's car was gone, but Juliette's was in the driveway. Hannah handed Petunia's leash to Samantha. "Can you put her in her pen? I want to talk to Juliette for a minute."

"Sure. I'll go back to the office in case you get held up here."

"Thanks. And, Samantha?"

"Uh-huh?"

"Make sure to close up the gate properly. I still haven't figured out how Petunia keeps escaping."

"Will do," Samantha replied before Petunia almost pulled her off her feet as she lurched toward her pen. "She must be ready for a beauty nap!"

Hannah let herself into Ruby's house. "Juliette? Are you here?"

No answer.

"I wonder where she's gotten herself to," Hannah said to the empty house.

Maisy ran to the door and jumped on Hannah's legs. She yipped and yapped as if she was telling an important story. "Is that so?" Hannah answered as she scooped Maisy into her arms and let the Moodle give her a kiss. "Where'd your momma get to without you?"

Hannah heard footsteps in the living room. "Hello? Juliette?"

Vanessa rounded the corner. "Oh. You startled me," she said to Hannah. "I was looking for Juliette, too, but I only found her dog. Or, I guess I should say that she found me."

"Juliette can't have gone far without Maisy," Hannah said. "I'll wait for her to get back." Hannah settled onto the couch and Maisy snuggled next to her. Hannah looked at Vanessa. "How did you get in the house?"

Vanessa sat across from Hannah. She flicked her wrist as if it was nothing. "Juliette asked me to meet her here. When she didn't answer, I tried the door and when it opened, I walked in thinking maybe she didn't hear me knock. No harm done." She checked her watch and twisted it around her wrist. "I guess I'll walk back to my cottage. Tell Juliette that I'm sorry I missed her."

A thump, thump, thump sounded from upstairs. Hannah jumped. Maisy leaped off the couch and ran barking toward the noise. Hannah followed. Maisy dashed up the stairs and stopped at the closed door to the room where Juliette was staying. She jumped on the door and scratched with both paws as the volume of her barking increased.

"What is it, Maisy?" Hannah reached for the doorknob.

As the door began to open, Hannah felt a hand on her back.

She turned her head expecting to see Vanessa peeking over her shoulder.

Vanessa was behind her but she didn't have a curious expression on her face; instead, it was twisted into a grimace. She shoved Hannah into the partly opened door which flew all the way open, sending Hannah sprawled on the floor.

Fortunately, Hannah's body responded even though her brain didn't have time to process what the heck was going on. She quickly rolled to her left a split second before a chair crashed on the spot where she had landed, only inches away from where she now lay, paralyzed with fear.

A thump brought her to life. From the floor she saw two feet tied together sticking out from under the bed. She scrambled to her feet as the bedroom door crashed closed.

"You have terrible timing, Hannah." Vanessa's muffled voice came through the locked door. "Don't disappear," Vanessa cackled. It sounded like she was fiddling with the doorknob. "I'll be back to deal with the two of you."

The two feet thrashed back and forth with increased intensity. Hannah pulled Juliette from under the bed. When their eyes met, Juliette relaxed.

Hannah tried to open the door but it wouldn't budge. "Vanessa likes rope, maybe she tied the door closed somehow. We'll figure that out after I get you freed."

Hannah quickly ripped the tape off Juliette's mouth and searched for something to cut through the rope tying her hands and feet.

"In my knitting bag. Scissors." Juliette's words came out in a jumble but Hannah got the message. She dumped the bag on the bed, on top of the finished hot pink blanket for Olivia, and found a small, but sharp, pair of scissors.

Sawing back and forth on the rope, Hannah desperately prayed for a miracle before Vanessa returned.

"She was so nice when she showed up at the front door," Juliette said. "She said she was walking on the beach and realized she needed to tell me something."

Hannah was only half-way through the rope, and the scissors were getting closer and closer to Juliette's wrist. She had to concentrate and be careful or else she might cut her. But that might be the least of their problems if Vanessa came back too soon. "She told you her real identity?"

"Only after she got me up here to show her the blanket I made for Olivia. It was all friendly chatter, a little bit about Monique and how much she missed her, how much she likes the beach, and how nice everyone has been to her. I actually felt sorry for her."

"She must have been plotting and planning this for the last six years. I was taken in by her phony stories, too."

"But you knew? About her being Candace?"

"Yes. She told me that Harold assaulted her and she needed to have plastic surgery. That she had tried to protect you and Monique. I didn't want to reveal her identity for fear that Harold would hurt her again. Wow, did I get *that* wrong." The ropes around Juliette's wrists fell away. "Finally."

Juliette massaged her wrists and flexed her fingers. "Thank you! I can feel my fingers again. Tingly but functional."

Footsteps outside the door made them both freeze. Hannah and Juliette stared at the doorknob. Someone jiggled it but it didn't open. Hannah heard muttering but no discernable words. More footsteps, but the sound clacked on the stairs and faded away.

Hannah wiped the sweat beading on her brow and sawed faster with the scissors on the rope around Juliette's ankles.

"Where's Maisy?" Juliette's voice carried a hint of panic. "Do you think that evil woman would hurt her?"

"She'll have a fight on her hands if she tries. Remember how Maisy bit Monique?"

Juliette giggled.

Hannah giggled too. Her nerves were about to burst but giggling relieved some of the tension. It also slowed down her work on the ropes. She pulled herself together, yanked hard on each side, but it didn't break. She had to cut more.

"Vanessa still thinks she can win Harold back. She thinks once I'm out of the way he'll need a shoulder to cry on and she actually thinks that shoulder will be hers," Juliette said.

"What about Gwen? She could still be competition for Vanessa." Hannah tried the rope again.

Juliette wiggled her feet and tried to stretch the rope. It was a bit looser. "Vanessa said Gwen is taken care of, too. I was the last piece she had to deal with; to get rid of." Juliette shuddered. "I regret wanting to find her to discuss Harold. That was a stupid plan on my part."

"That was your unfinished business?"

Juliette nodded.

Hannah looked at Juliette. "Gwen called me, terrified. She said Colin told her she was in danger and he's hiding her someplace."

Juliette's face paled. "While Vanessa tied me up, she bragged that Colin was working with her. All she had to do was bribe him with some money."

CHAPTER 27

Hannah made two more sawing motions with the scissors, and with Juliette keeping tension on the rope, it finally broke apart. She scrambled to her feet.

Yipping and yapping filtered through the bedroom window. Juliette rushed to see what was happening. She made a circular motion with her hand behind her back. "Hannah, get over here. Quick!"

Hannah and Juliette stared out the bedroom window right into Petunia's pen. Maisy, the ten pound Moodle, had her front paws on the gate and used her nose to push the latch up and out of its proper position. She dropped to the ground and the gate swung open.

"That clever little stinker," Juliette said with pride dripping from her words.

Petunia walked through the gate as if she was on a fashion show runway, looking left and right. The Moodle, with the potbelly pig trotting behind, moved out of view of the window.

Juliette looked at Hannah. "What now?" she whispered.

They didn't have to wait for long. Noise from the other side of the bedroom door drew their attention back inside.

Hannah scanned the bedroom for anything that could be used as a weapon. She picked up the heaviest book on the bookshelf and noiselessly moved to the side of the door and motioned for Juliette to do the same. Juliette armed herself with her scissors.

They waited motionless for what felt like an eternity but nothing happened.

Voices filtered into the bedroom but Hannah couldn't understand any words. Was someone talking to Vanessa?

Suddenly, the clomp, clomp of heavy shoes running up the stairs rang through the house. Someone pulled on the door until it flew open. Hannah had her book ready.

"Jack?" Hannah's arms fell to her sides and the book dropped to the floor with a loud thud. Juliette still held the scissors in front of her. Jack carefully relieved her of her weapon.

"Are you two all right?" Jack's eyes searched Hannah up and down before he did the same to Juliette.

Pam, Samantha, and Ruby crowded into the room.

Like a bullet, Maisy dove through all the legs and leaped up into Juliette's arms, kissing her face until Juliette laughed and fell on the bed.

"Where's Vanessa?" Hannah asked.

"Don't worry about her. She's locked up tight in my police car, ready for a little trip to a secure facility. Along with her partner."

"Colin?"

"Uh-huh. He spilled the beans as soon as I pulled into the driveway behind his Mustang," Pam explained. "It's a good thing you called me or you two might have ended up as fish bait. Vanessa had a boat all ready to go to dump your bodies out to sea."

"That must have been why Colin was hiding out near the marina. Did he really plan to let Vanessa get rid of Gwen?" Hannah asked.

"Nope. He had a big change of heart but he is still in trouble for dismantling the security camera for Vanessa and hiding the fact that she was the one who pushed Monique into the pool."

"Geesh." Hannah shook her head. "Vanessa is one sick woman. She was actually delusional enough to want Harold back. And to think he'd want her back, too. Does Harold know about any of this yet?"

"He showed up after I had Colin in custody. I don't know how he knew where to go." Pam gave Hannah a glare from the corner of her eye but kept what she was thinking to herself.

Jack put his arm around Hannah. "So Petunia escaped again and she dragged Maisy along to get help. Can you believe it?"

Hannah laughed and looked at Juliette. "Well, that's not exactly what happened. We watched Maisy from the bedroom window as she opened the latch on the gate and led Petunia out of the back-yard. We didn't know where they were going, but Maisy was definitely in charge. Is Petunia back in her pen?"

"She is, but I'd better add a different latch if Maisy is going to be around for a lengthy visit," Jack said.

"About that." Juliette put her hand on Ruby's arm. "Do you think Olivia could take care of Maisy for me? I've decided to do some traveling."

"Are you serious? Olivia is madly in love with Maisy and I think it's mutual. She couldn't have a better home away from home. Olivia's downstairs with her treasure box, why don't you go give her the good news."

Juliette picked up the hot pink knitted blanket. "I finished this, too. Should I wrap it up?"

Ruby stroked the soft yarn. "It's beautiful. Why don't you wrap Maisy up in it and put them both in Olivia's lap?"

Juliette took Ruby's advice. All that showed of the Moodle was her white head and bright black eyes sticking out of the blanket. The color suited her perfectly.

Jack followed them down the stairs, leaving Hannah and Pam in Juliette's room.

"You can stop by the police station tomorrow and give me your statement. I've got enough to do now with Vanessa and

Colin in custody," Pam said. She stared out the bedroom window. "I don't suppose my father has shared anything with you yet?"

"Not yet."

Pam sighed. "I wish he wasn't such a stubborn curmudgeon but I think he's too old to change."

"I'll agree with that."

Hannah followed Pam downstairs. Olivia cuddled Maisy while Juliette told Ruby everything that happened with Vanessa. Hannah let herself out and walked to the beach. She was more than ready for a quiet walk back to her place.

The waves rushed over the sand, almost licking her feet. It was a good feeling to know that some things never changed.

Cal was waiting on Hannah's porch with his long legs perched on the railing. He held his arms out and Hannah fell into his lap. She inhaled his woodsy, salty scent. "Before you say anything, I only went to Ruby's house. How could I know that Vanessa was ready to murder Juliette and I stumbled into her plan?"

Cal stroked Hannah's long braid and wrapped his arms around her a little tighter. "Ruby called me. I heard Petunia and Maisy were the heroes."

Hannah snickered. "Not exactly. Gwen's phone call to me asking for help set everything in motion, but Maisy and Petunia brought in the reinforcements."

"How about I get the burgers out of your fridge and bring them to my boat for dinner. I'll pick up wine and beer and some salad, too."

"That sounds perfect. After I take a shower, I'll swing by."

"Okay."

They snuggled for a while before Cal left.

By the time Hannah stepped into her shower, she was more than ready for the hot water to wash away the day's grime and everything else—fear, worry, and her anxiety circled the drain and disappeared, too.

Hannah had one stop to make before she joined Cal on his

boat. She turned her Volvo station wagon into the driveway behind the tidy cedar shingled cottage with a view of the ocean. As she walked around the side of the cottage she heard two voices.

"We should spend more time together."

"You are a stubborn son-of-a-gun sometimes, Jack. What did it take for you to finally reach that conclusion? Expecting a death sentence in that lab report?" Caroline scolded.

Hannah slowed her pace and heard one last comment. "I'm already dead," Caroline joked, "but I'm glad you got a clean bill of health."

Hannah coughed to give them a warning.

"Hannah? Get over here so I can touch you. Jack just told me what happened and I can't bear to think that miserable woman even considered harming you. And we all thought the bad guy was Harold."

"I don't think he's exactly a good guy, but he's not a murderer," Hannah said as she scooched in between two of her favorite people. She looked at Jack. "Did you tell Pam about the results yet? She's going out of her mind worrying about you."

"Women!" Jack squeezed Hannah's knee. "I called her on my way over here. I knew I would never hear the last of it if I didn't tell Pam first. But I still think you all should worry more about yourselves and less about an old curmudgeon like me."

Hannah smiled and put one arm around Jack and the other around Caroline.

The twinkle was back in Jack's eyes when he grinned at her.

This is the end of Caught Dead Handed. I hope you enjoyed the story. Click here and start reading my next book today!

A NOTE FROM LYNDSEY

Thank you for reading my cozy mystery, *Caught Dead Handed.*
Never miss a release date and sign up for my newsletter here
—http://LyndseyColeBooks.com

ABOUT THE AUTHOR

Lyndsey Cole lives in New England in a small rural town with her husband who puts up with all the characters in her head, her dog who hogs the couch, her cat who is the boss, and 3 chickens that would like to move into the house. She surrounds herself with gardens full of beautiful perennials. Sitting among the flowers with the scent of lilac, peonies, lily of the valley, or whatever is in bloom, stimulates her imagination about who will die next!

ALSO BY LYNDSEY COLE

The Hooked & Cooked Series

Gunpowder Chowder

Mobsters and Lobsters

A Fishy Dish

Crook, Line and Sinker

Catch of the Dead

Lily Bloom Series

Begonia Means Beware

Queen of Poison

Roses are Dead

Drowning in Dahlias

Hidden by the Hydrangeas

Christmas Tree Catastrophe

The Black Cat Café Series

BlueBuried Muffins

StrawBuried in Chocolate

BlackBuried Pie

Very Buried Cheesecake

RaspBuried Torte

PoisonBuried Punch

CranBuried Coffee Cake

WineBuried Wedding

<u>Jingle Buried Cookies</u>

<u>Easter Buried Eggs</u>

.

Made in the USA
Coppell, TX
02 October 2021